PRINCIPLES OF UNCERTAINTY AND OTHER CONSTANTS

Principles of Uncertainty and Other Constants

Stories by Mitch Levenberg

Mitch Levenberg

Principles of Uncertainty and Other Constants
Stories by Mitch Levenberg

iUniverse books may be ordered through booksellers or by contacting:

iUniverse
1663 Liberty Drive
Bloomington, IN 47403
www.iuniverse.com
844-349-9409

ISBN: 978-0-5953-7834-0 (sc)

Print information available on the last page.

iUniverse rev. date: 07/23/2020

To my wife Julie and daughter Anna Rose without whom this, as well as many other endeavors, would have little meaning.

To my friend Salvatore Salamone without whom this book would be full of wrong choices, not to mention a lot of typos.

To my friend Mark Goldblatt for his introduction and for his continual over-praising of my talents.

To my friend John LiCastro with whose help and encouragement I am continuously able to see the world for the whacky place it really is.

To my Mother and Father without whom I really wouldn't have been able to do this at all.

ACKNOWLEDGEMENTS

1. "The Package"(2006)   The St. Ann's Review

2. "The Cat" (2004)   How Not To Greet Famous People: the best stories from Ducts.org

3. "The Bagel King" (1993)   Confluence

4. "The Hotel Clerk" (1992)   The New Delta Review

5. "Placenta"(1992)   The Ledge

6. "Telepathy" (1991)   The Ledge

7. "Soup" (1990)   Fiction

8. "Sidera" (1989)   Fine Madness

9. "Alaska" (1988)   The Beacon Review

10. "The Key Chain" (1988)   Fine Madness

11. "The Cruller" (1988)   Fiction

C O N T E N T S

▼

Introduction

The typical Levenberg tale begins with an ontological quirk, a sudden rift in the relationship of cause and effect into which the hapless but hopeful protagonist feels himself drawn. Jogging around a stagnant lake, a lonely man encounters a beautiful young woman peering into the souls of dead fish. Killing time at an inexplicably menacing greasy spoon, a jittery diner gets caught up in the sexually-charged psychodrama between a wise-cracking waitress and the foul-mouthed brute working the register. Hearing two men arguing violently in the street below, a bookish tenant reflexively buzzes them into his apartment.

That's when things get *really* weird.

What holds these stories together, what makes them performance pieces beyond their literary value, is the language. "The Cat," for example, contains this passage: "Then he took out his knife, brandished it round the apartment for a while and said, 'Now what do you got around here that I can cut up?' I thought about the cat my neighbor left here for the weekend so he could go upstate and visit his girlfriend. I thought about all those girlfriends who for some reason or other live upstate and how now a cat was going to die for it." The nightmarish slapstick is conveyed through a perfect inversion of form and content, deadpan prose and deadly subject matter.

"The Hotel Clerk" begins with a paranoid jewel of a sentence: "There was something horrible about Germans laughing at the top of their lungs and him not able to get the jokes." When the Jewish narrator confesses to a seductive German hotel clerk that he does not have an itinerary for the day, she replies, "You must then go to Dachau." She means, of course, he should take time to visit the notorious concentration camp. Or does she? Is she reminding him to pay his respects to the horror done to his people, or is she reminding him who he is, where he is, and what might happen to him if he doesn't watch out?

In "Telepathy," the protagonist moves in with a woman named Telepathy—one of several Levenberg-ian title-characters/love-interests whose names suggest a predicament: "Placenta," "Dyspnea," "Alaska." Telepathy is both graced with and afflicted by the gift her name suggests, a point the narrator accepts immediately and unquestioningly. Their romance follows perfectly from the logic of their circumstance: "'Well, aren't you in a foul mood,' she'd say to me just as I was opening my eyes that day for the first time. Sometimes I'd go back to sleep and ask her to wake me up when she thought I was in a better mood." Later, to save their relationship, they agree to think like one another; he, "to look deeply into the secret nature of things," and she, to see only what's visible, to dwell on surfaces. But neither can pull it off. Then the doorbell rings. He has no idea who or what waits on the other side of the door; she claims not to know either: "But I knew she was lying. She too had struggled all day, not to know as I did, but to unknow, to see nothing, to know nothing past the first unsuspecting moments of the day. But she too had failed. I saw that. In the normal unempathetic way of humans figuring things out, I truly knew that."

What waits on the other side of the door is what inevitably waits on the other side of the door.

The end of the story.

Read these stories to their ends. This is literature. The real deal.

—Mark Goldblatt, 2006

DREAM OF THE CHINESE RAILROAD OFFICIAL

He yelled at me so hard for a few moments I didn't think it was me at all he was talking to, but some abstraction, like in a dream, into a mirror perhaps, my face the mirror of who he thinks he is, he the mirror of who I think he is—but who is he really?

He was so close I felt the heat of his breath, his entire lunch, every meal really he may have ever chewed, layers upon layers came pouring out at me. Apparently, I had done something wrong. I was sure of it. He said so, not in so many words, but in the way his eyes tore into me, tore me to shreds without his having to lift a finger. I don't remember his fingers, per se, not apart from his hands, yes, peripherally of course; I didn't dare take my eyes off his face, but every so often his hands would rise to face level, his, mine, both of ours, and I would flinch at first, expecting to be struck, but after a while saw his hands only as instruments of instruction and explanation, and a way of emphasizing his words which were incomprehensible to me yet, nevertheless, I could deeply appreciate.

In a short while, he was joined by a woman also wearing a railroad official uniform—she mostly nodded her head, first in the affirmative, then in the negative, up and down, then sideways, then up and down, like a puppet controlled by hidden strings, perhaps his own, as if to say, yes, he's right, you are a scoundrel and an outlaw and must be dealt with accordingly, but carefully, discreetly; after all there were people watching—yes, actually watching, enjoying the whole scene, even laughing at times, nervously, of course, because they knew it could happen to them, and occasionally the woman would shake her head yes, as if I had asked a question, which I hadn't or at least didn't remember doing so, like "Am I in some kind of trouble?" and she would keep nodding up and down like she was agreeing to the following statements made by the male official: "You are irredeemable. There is no chance for forgiveness. You must not try to defend yourself, not in the slightest. Your paperwork is not in order and never will be. Your face is the face of a hopeless criminal and always will be."

I said nothing to all this. I just took it all in, figuring it would all have to stop sometime, somewhere down the line; for example, a train was due any minute. I had a ticket for it and if I remembered correctly, it was stamped with today's date. The only problem was what was today's date and also, of course, where was the ticket because when I went through my pockets, which the official strongly objected to, thinking I was searching for a weapon, and thus, threatened to take me away for good, I found no ticket, anywhere and was convinced, along with everything else, my pockets had been picked. The train was coming from Shanghai. It was affectionately known, in some circles, as the Shanghai Express. Perhaps, if I was lucky, he would put me on that train, thinking it was some kind of punishment, a type of exile from where we were now, the name of which slipped my mind, but perhaps, I thought, and again to my credit, forgetting where I was might be interpreted as a sign I mean no harm, that one place is as good as the next and I could easily, comfortably, be somewhere else as here. But he would have known of that. I also had this uncomfortable, really nagging feeling that the train had already come and gone and no other trains were coming that day, that all trains had been temporarily stopped, for a thousand years or more, because of me. The track looked endless, vast, empty, void of all meaning and purpose, just tracks for tracks sake. Nothing coming, nothing as far as the eye could see.

And now my eyes had to see only this man's face. They had no other choice. It was either an endless, meaningless void or this man's face that at least had substance, meaning, as bad as it might be. I remember the saliva foaming outside his mouth like a mad dog. Yes, perhaps he was a mad dog who I chose to make into a railroad official.

And the woman? She had weasel-like features and at the very most she was a mad weasel. She was still there. Just quiet, nodding and shaking her head a lot. Someone who seemed to want a bigger part in the matter, yet knew her place and perhaps was even grateful she had been allowed to be part of this at all, had been promoted to nodding and shaking of the head status, no mean promotion at that. You couldn't fault her. I had a feeling she had been an orphan; perhaps it was because she was missing some fingers and had a cleft palate, so that she had to feel fortunate she had made it this far in life.

I didn't mind looking at her as much as I did the male RR official. I thought, in some twisted way, that this woman may even have been the daughter I never adopted. The one left behind and now she was getting even with me. As for the man, he was no orphan. He was more what orphans dread, their worst nightmare. And yet, I knew he was just doing his job, that he was being a bit overzealous because he had to be a mentor you might say for the woman, a terrifying example to the people surrounding us, and perhaps, finally, he feared that among these innocent looking people lurked a spy from the local government or the committee of RR officials. I doubt, whatever the case, he was paid enough.

Regardless, I was suffering in his wake. He was like some tub of acid that kept spilling over, threatening to engulf me like some freak industrial accident waiting to happen. Then, she, she of the nodding head, a disgruntled orphan, began to take on this disgusted, dismissive smirk which slowly, methodically began to destroy me, first my heart, then my soul. I thought of my own daughter one day, going out to all hours of the night, not telling me where she's been, bringing back horrible men with their shirts unbuttoned and their flies half open. I wanted her gone. The man was out there, pure over the top anger, but she, she was far more subtle, so far more disturbing. There was something about her...something about her, which I couldn't quite wrap my mind around.

I thought of actually pushing her away, and the moment I thought it, she actually began to stumble backwards, to lose her balance, to have to be caught by the crowd before falling onto the tracks. But it wasn't me, it was him, because suddenly, the man had begun waving his arms as well as his hands so that at one point he had struck the woman on his back swing while making a point. He never looked back at her as she stumbled and nearly fell onto the tracks.

She didn't matter. He just kept screaming and screaming until he stopped as quickly as he had begun, just stopped and stared at me, turning now a very deep shade of purple. I thought at first it was caused by the shadows of the receding day, a simple play of light and dark rather than anything internal like a heart attack or stroke. Perhaps he was pausing just long enough for me to finally speak or to remain quiet, pausing to make sure I knew enough to keep quiet even if I had the opportunity to speak.

Of course I said nothing. What could I say? I only knew enough Chinese to say "How are you?" "I love you," or "Goodbye" none of which seemed appropriate here. Nevertheless, I felt myself starting to say something. My voice seemed deep inside me, cowering behind my heart or small intestines or some other twisted irrelevant organ, but suddenly there it was, moving to the forefront, traveling on some sort of bus through my body, over rough and unpredictable terrain, through the dark, gravelly tunnel of my throat and at last into the purple light of the official's face.

I spoke to him. Yes, later, years later, lying on my back in some strange city, trying to get back home to someplace, this is what they told me I said: "I think you made your point." Those were the words I seemed to have uttered, not in a sarcastic or even ironic way, but quite seriously. I don't think I wanted him to die and yet that purple pallor, deepening by the moment might, in the long run, mean nothing less than sudden, or almost sudden, death. No, I didn't want him to die, so I wanted him to know he had made his point and I would not do whatever it was I was supposed to have done again.

In a way, I was becoming fond of him. He reminded me of someone I knew and might at one time have respected, admired for his courage and perseverance, not to mention his incredible conviction and resolve. All of that despite being wrong. He was everything I wanted to be. His willingness to die to make a point was outstanding, though entirely unnecessary.

So I said, "I think you made your point," not like I knew he did, not that there was any conviction in what I said, only that I said it quite sincerely, as if I meant it, though it was bound to be misinterpreted, because anything I said now would necessarily be misinterpreted unless it was an outright confession of wrongdoing. Yet, even that wouldn't end this, because it really didn't matter whether I admitted to any wrongdoing or not since why should he believe me either way.

No, it was enough that he knew I had done something wrong; I was completely out of this; my opinion was not solicited, only my presence would be tolerated in the most intolerable way. All that mattered to him was the accusation itself, the actual measure of it, its weight,depth, length,width, etc. until he either ran out of things to say, (but even those things would be repeated over and over) or else he would die doing it, which would be a great service to his country. Certainly, I envied him, this great commitment to pure, unadulterated anger. There would be no more or less anger on his part whether I had committed one wrongdoing or every wrongdoing the world had ever seen.

Yes, I was envious. I stood there in the middle of a blazing hot afternoon on a RR platform in China, being excoriated, lacerated, humiliated, dehumanized by some guy I had never seen before yet felt I knew all my life. And, of course, I envied his ability to do that. That's when I began to imagine I was him. In a way, of course I was him. We were two sides of the same coin, one side angry, aggressive, irrational, relentless, the other passive, weak, frightened. Yes, I began slowly, and then suddenly to realize that the only way out of this was to see myself as him, to be him. I began to feel his power, his anger wash over me like some nerve tingling balm. "What fucking nerve," yes, that very phrase came into my head when for the longest time not very much was coming into my head at all. I felt my heart start beating hard against my chest like just before some potentially dramatic, if not violent confrontation. I felt the sweat burning my eyes and saw things I had not seen before like a RR ticket sticking out of the official's pocket, a set of keys hanging from his trousers, his cap that was so oversized he had to keep pushing it back from his eyes, the sweat pouring down from his forehead, independent of his will.

In other words, he began to look very ordinary, foolish even. His teeth were yellow and crooked, his breath smelled badly of fish, a mole suddenly appeared at the corner of his mouth which seemed to dance wildly when he shouted. This last thing made me smile and finally laugh. I couldn't stop laughing. Of course, he began to scream even louder but the louder he screamed, the louder I laughed, and soon I noticed how the muscles in his face began to outstretch themselves until they collapsed into a sagging heap.

Suddenly, I saw a pathetic old man, the remains only of a RR official. I noticed now how his uniform, like his cap, started to look too big on him so that while one hand waved rather weakly at me, the other was trying to hold up his pants. I felt sorry for him. I wanted to help him now. "You're right!" I screamed back at him. "I was wrong! I merit no forgiveness! I deserve only the harshest punishment!" But these words, shouted into his face like that, only made him back off in terror. He looked at me now with a terrible, shocking recognition, as if in me he saw himself, saw something too terrifying to acknowledge, as if somehow I was real and he wasn't, that all along he had only been a terrifying figment of my imagination.

But before he could either utter another word or just stand there saying nothing, the woman pushed him out of the way, pushed him so hard he tumbled onto the tracks. No one tried to catch him. They all just let him go. He had outgrown his usefulness.

"Dad!" I cried out to him. "Dad, watch out!" But it was too late.

Then the woman looked at me with great scorn. I expected nothing less, but before she too could utter a single word, there came the sound of a train heading towards us. She seemed as surprised as I did. When she turned around to watch it coming, way in the distance, I bent down to pick up my suitcase. Of course it wasn't there. It was never there. But I made the gesture and that's all that seemed important at the moment.

Soup

As soon as he got to Florida, he stopped for soup. He had been stopping for soup constantly since he left New York. He was craving soup a lot lately, but he knew that if he had it every time he craved it, he'd have to recognize it as something abnormal, an obsession perhaps, something that might eventually affect his ability to function in the real world. So he decided he'd have soup only at certain intervals, at every certain number of miles, rather than whenever he craved it. First it was every three hundred miles, then two hundred, and finally he'd let himself stop for soup every hundred miles until he got home.

There was one exception he could remember, however, and that was when he had reached his ninetieth mile between soups and noticed a restaurant off the road that boasted of the best New England clam chowder in the county. He forgot the name of the county but he still remembered the soup.

"God, that was delicious," he thought. That was the best New England clam chowder I ever had, and that includes New England, he decided. He thought it might have been in North Carolina, or was it in South Carolina? It got confusing because it just as well have been South Carolina when he was traveling north, or North Carolina when he was traveling south. From now on, he thought, he might keep records. At least of the name of the county, state, restaurant, and type of soup, and maybe the names of those waitresses who were nice to him and those who weren't.

Once he came to a place that claimed to have the best chicken soup in North America, and it was there that he became involved with the waitress.

When he sat down at the counter, even before he ordered the soup the wait-ress said, "You're not from around here, are you?" This prompted him to turn around as if expecting an attack from the rear.

"What do you mean?" he asked.

"Just that," she said. "I have no ulterior motives, if that's what you think."

She said "ulterior motives" with the kind of vocal stress and elevation one might reserve for children or deaf people, as if she had just learned its meaning and was trying it out for the first time.

"Actually," he told her, "I live not more than three hundred miles south of here, in Fort Lauderdale."

"Yeah, but you're not really from here," she said. "I mean not originally."

She pronounced "originally" with the same wide-mouthed emphasis as she did "ulterior motives." He noticed how her teeth resembled the Formica counter with its occasional yellow stains and chipped surfaces.

"I'm from New York originally," he told her. He did all he could not to over-emphasize the word "originally," worried it might come off as mimicking her.

"I knew it!" she said. "I knew it!" she said as if she had won some kind of con-test, and he knew this would be just the thing to set one of these people off. He knew he had to calm her down, quickly change the subject before she told every-one in the restaurant how she guessed he was from somewhere else.

"I bet you that chicken soup isn't as good as you say it is," he challenged.

She stopped smiling. "I bet you it is," she said.

"Well," he said. "I won't be able to tell until I taste it, will I?"

"Is that your negative New York way of ordering a bowl?" she asked him.

He laughed. He was wrong. She wasn't one of those kinds of people. She was a lot shrewder than what he took her for and at the same time her eyes were the brightest he had ever seen, almost liquidy like corn soup, and all he knew was that right now he wanted her to keep looking at him.

"Sorry," he said. "I suppose I've gotten a little cynical in my search for the per-fect soup."

This confused and impressed her at the same time. She loved the way he spoke, but nothing he said seemed to make any sense.

"Is that right?" she said in a slightly exaggerated accent, again as if she might be speaking to a small child speaking a lot of gibberish. That indicated right away that she liked him but wasn't taking him very seriously.

"That's right," he said, trying to mimic her but failing because of his northern self-consciousness.

"You got nice blue eyes," she told him. "Northern blue, am I right?"

"You're right," he said. "And yours are cornfield yellow, right?"

"I don't know," she said. "They change in the light. Anyway, let me get you that soup."

As she walked away, he wondered how he might sneak her out of here without anyone noticing. Not that he wished to kidnap her, stash her in his trunk or anything like that, but he thought he might like to spend some time with her, maybe have a picnic in the municipal park in town. When she came back with the soup, she warned him not to touch the bowl straight off since it was too hot, even though she herself had her hands firmly wrapped around it. She could handle the hot stuff all right, no doubt about that. Here was the blood-and-guts demeanor of the southern waitress he had often thought about as well as seen in the movies, willing to sacrifice her own hands to get the job done. Maybe she was, in the long run, despite her bright, translucent eyes, too tough for him. Indeed, he noticed no change at all in her expression as she freed her hands from the bowl and placed it carefully, not a drop spilled, in front of him.

"When do you think would be the right time to touch it?" he asked her.

"Let the soup cool first," she advised him, as if reading off the first in a long list of rules on how to eat soup. "You don't want to burn your tongue, do you?" she asked him; the question was as hot as the soup itself and its implications excited him.

And the soup did appear very hot. Too hot to eat. The smoke rose so high and was so thick he had trouble seeing her now behind the counter. Still, he was pleased to find he could see her eyes burning like the headlights of a car through a curtain of dense fog.

"Why so hot, then?" he asked her through the curtain.

"Gotta make sure the chicken's dead," she said.

He hadn't even tasted the soup and yet he felt he had known her for a long time. Perhaps now, between the soup's cooling and his eating it, he should make his move. No, he thought. Eat the soup first. So he let it cool, and when there was but the smallest trace of smoke still rising from the bowl, he lifted his spoon.

"I think I'm ready," he told her.

She looked back at him and smiled from the grill, where she was making hamburgers for some truck drivers. This frightened him. He tasted the soup, but it was still too hot and he ended up burning his tongue just as she warned him he might. So there was nothing behind that burning question after all he thought.

"How is it?" she asked.

"Good," he lied. For as soon as he could taste it, he realized it was all a lie, that this was nothing but soup from a can.

"You don't like it, do you?" she asked.

"I like you a lot better," he said softly so the truck drivers couldn't hear him.

"What?" she said. But he didn't repeat it. Instead he asked for salt. She handed him the salt and he poured it into his soup, but both of them knew it was too late, that nothing could save it. She no longer smiled. He could see how disappointed she was, far more than he was.

"Look," he said. "It's not your fault. Just because the place serves soup from a can, it doesn't mean that you yourself are a worthless person."

"Do you really think so?" she asked.

"Yes," he said.

"I used to be smart," she said, before I came to work here. I thought maybe I'd go to college one day, but you know how it is. You make all these plans and then just get into a rut and before you know it, you're dead."

"Yes," he said. "I do."

"Well, that's what happened to me, I guess."

He took another spoonful of soup for her sake. Now it was too cold to eat. He noticed the truck drivers get up and leave. He wondered how much of him they noticed and whether they might be planning something for him outside. He decided he wouldn't move until their trucks moved out.

"What do you do?" she suddenly asked him. This question always threw him; he knew that as long as he lived, and no matter what he did, he'd never like it.

"I teach college," he said.

"College!" she exclaimed. "You teach college," she told him as if he himself might be learning it for the first time.

"Yes," he said. "At a very small college in south Florida."

"A professor," she said to herself. "I can't believe I'm serving soup to a professor."

"You're making far too much of this," he said. He didn't want her to put any more distance between them than was absolutely necessary. "It's really not a big thing."

"Oh, but it is," she insisted. "I've never met a professor before. In fact, I've never met anyone very smart before. Oh, God you must know so much. This is so exciting!" On the other hand, he thought, maybe this was working to his advantage.

"Please," he said. "You're embarrassing me."

"What are you doing here?" she asked.

"I was up North visiting my mother," he told her. "And now I'm on my way back…"

"And you just happened to walk in here for soup, right?"

"Right," he said.

"How long you gonna be in town for?" she asked him.

"Just until I finish this soup," he answered.

"That's not very long, is it?" she asked.

"Not unless you'd like to reheat it for me," he told her.

"You know," she said. "If you wanted to hang around for a few hours I could give you some soup at home a lot better than this."

Homemade soup, he thought. What could be better than that, except what could she possibly know about homemade soup? Could she be more than twenty years old, he wondered.

"You mean you're going to make your mother sweat over a hot stove just for me?" he asked.

"I live alone," she said

"Anything to do around here while I'm waiting?" he asked.

"There's a park," she said. "And a movie theater. Also an aquarium and the library. It's not Sea World or anything but it's got some exotic fish in it."

First he went to the park. He was feeling very tired now from a combination of things. There was all the driving he had done and then the soup which had made him lethargic and most of all the strain of talking to the waitress. Perhaps he would sit on one of the benches and take a nap. But just as he was about to close his eyes he noticed two squirrels fighting in front of him. They seemed pretty serious as if they intended to rip each other apart and with squirrels you never knew. What was he supposed to do? Pull them apart? Ignore them? Lecture them on the rules of park etiquette? For god's sake, he thought. They're just squirrels doing squirrel things, let it go.

As far as he knew all this tearing each other apart could just be part of the natural order of things. He suddenly realized how little he really knew about the animal kingdom. He picked up a pebble and threw it behind him, hoping to cause a distraction. It didn't work, however, and they remained locked in mortal combat or whatever ritual they were involved in and he knew only a rifle blast could ever really separate them.

Perhaps this tearing at each other was merely some animal foreplay before making love, especially the human animal, he thought as he sat in the park waiting till the waitress got off. It was hard to imagine that only hours from now, he and the waitress might be ripping into each other just like this in some forbidden ritual of love where only a rifle blast could separate them.

That's what he was afraid of. What was he letting himself in for? Pretty much the same thing as the squirrels, he thought, although he'd rather think it was his desire for homemade soup rather than young female flesh that was really keeping him here. Either way he was an outsider, someone only wanting to bring shame and scandal to a small sleepy southern town—that would be so unlike him.

He was feeling guiltier by the minute. So he would leave the park. Certainly the squirrels didn't want him. The small children playing on the swings and monkey bars didn't want him, nor did their mothers, who looked over at him from time to time as if he meant to harm them or their children.

There was a time he only kept his mind on reaching home. When he proceeded in a linear direction, he was a man with a purpose, but once he stopped, stopped any time longer than it took to eat his soup and get back in the car, once he began to make small circular motions, to roam the streets of a small town waiting for a young waitress to get off from work, he was no better than a drifter, a man with no set goals or purpose, a dangerous element to himself and to society.

His next stop was the town aquarium, which was behind the library. It consisted of two large fish tanks which he thought were shaped remarkably like fish bowls. "Seafood soup," he said to himself. "Living breathing seafood soup, and no doubt the best in town."

Indeed, the inhabitants of that soup were exotic fish, though how exotic he couldn't tell; certainly they were a lot more exotic than the people who put them in the bowls. There were bloated green fish and triangular orange ones and large-lipped, pencil-thin pink ones which occasionally smacked against the side of the tank as if they meant to attack him. He wondered if anyone had noticed that. Even the fish in this town didn't trust him. All they did was circle each other as if looking for something but never getting the message that there was nothing there. First the animal kingdom would smell him out, then the humans would. He knew the pattern. Sitting next to the last fish tank was a three-hundred pound boy who held a donation box in his hands. He knew he would have to give enough money to pass by and get out alive. "This is the one they'll send after me if things get out of hand," he said to himself.

There were only two more hours before the waitress left work, and he thought he might go to the movies. Certainly, he thought, this would be a good way to spend the rest of the time, especially to keep out of people's sight for a while. His craving for soup was growing again, and if it had no eating scenes, a movie would be a good distraction.

He had come in the middle, and fearful of sitting in someone's lap because it was so dark, he stood in the center aisle. And what if, what if the lights suddenly went on and everyone saw him there, standing alone, purposeless in the middle aisle of the movie theatre, what then? But when his eyes adjusted, and he finally could make out the seats, he noticed the theater was practically empty and most, if not all his fears dissipated. However, it was quite likely, he thought, that all the eyes which had long since become adjusted had been looking at him as he stood foolish and helpless in the center aisle.

"You're being paranoid," he said to himself. "This is Florida. Your adopted state. Just relax and watch the movie." He sat down at the end of a row near the center aisle so he could make a quick getaway once the movie ended. The movie itself seemed to focus on two people, a man and woman slightly younger than he, who were traveling by car through a desert. In the scene he was watching, their car had broken down. It was very hot and neither the man nor the woman seemed to be wearing very much.

More often than not, he was more influenced by the climactic conditions on the screen than in the theater; he was starting to get very thirsty watching the two people sweating in the desert. Every time they took a swig of water out of their canteen he grew more envious and yearned for the sensation they were experiencing. During one such swig, he finally decided to get up and go to the water fountain in the lobby, but before reaching it he noticed the candy counter.

Behind the counter was a woman who could have doubled for the woman in the movie except that she was much younger. At the moment, she was doing her best to deflect certain advances being thrust upon her by a tall thin boy around her age who also worked in the theater but was obviously neglecting his job.

"Y'all better sweep out that lobby before Mr. Johnson gets back," she warned him.

Mr. Johnson must be the manager, he figured, a man who seemed to strike terror in both of them. Even he didn't like the sound of this Mr. Johnson, whom he pictured with steel-framed glasses and a bow tie—he no doubt ordered the patrons around as well as the workers. The boy picked up his broom and dragged himself back to sweeping. Now the girl was alone.

"Do you sell soda?" he asked her.

"Of course we sell soda," she told him. "What movie theater doesn't sell soda?" she asked.

"You'd be surprised," he told her, knowing full well that even he would be surprised at such a possibility. He would have thought she'd come across all types in her job, but this town didn't have more than one or two types.

"What country you from?" she asked him.

"From this country," he said. "Florida, U.S.A."

"No kidding?" she asked.

"No kidding," he said. "Ya coulda fooled me," she said.

The boy had stopped sweeping and was looking over at him.

"Then how come you don't know we sell soda in all the movie theaters around here?"

It would take something just like this, he thought, to get someone like this started. How often did anyone say anything out of the ordinary in this town, he wondered, and how often would it be tolerated?

"I did know," he said "I was only fooling with you," he said.

"I don't know," she said. "I think you're from another country and you just ain't tellin'. That's what I think."

He didn't like the way the boy had suddenly stopped sweeping in order to listen to his conversation with the girl, especially with Mr. Johnson looming somewhere in the background. He thought about getting his soda quickly and then getting lost in the darkness of the theater—who knew what the boy might be planning—but at the same time he wanted to stay where he was, talking to the girl. He liked her; he wanted to keep talking to her. Then he wondered if maybe she'd like to sit and watch the rest of the movie with him. He liked the idea she looked like the woman in the film, and this certainly would add to the excitement of sitting next to her.

He and his wife used to go to the movies all the time; now they hardly went at all, and when they did they sat together like strangers with their coats between them. She didn't like him to touch her because it distracted her attention from the film. He wanted to go back to an earlier time when he could touch and be touched by a woman in the theater and enjoy the movie at the same time. It was those damn art movies that were killing his marriage, the ones where you had to concentrate on reading the subtitles or listening to the intricate subtleties of the dialogue. Passion was reserved for the characters on the screen: they were real and you were not.

Once during a Bergman film he dared to reach across the coats for his wife's hand. She quickly pulled it away and then said to him, "Are you interested in me or the film?" to which he replied, "Sorry, it won't happen again."

And it didn't. And now he wondered if this girl who thought he was from a foreign country would agree to sit next to him in the movie theater.

"Actually, I'm from New York," he dared to tell her. "I moved here to Florida a few years ago for a job," he told her.

"What do y'all do?" she asked.

"I'm a teacher," he said. "A college teacher."

"You mean like a professor?" she asked.

"That's right," he said proudly, "a college professor."

"Then what are y'all doing here?" she asked.

That was a good question. What was he doing here? Certainly, he didn't belong here. How can you belong to a place, he thought, when you always have to justify being there, even to yourself?

Even his mother went back home. Once his father died, his mother took his body and flew home with it and never came back. She told him she wanted to die in the same place she was born and of course be near his father's grave. That was okay. She was just returning to the Jewish graveyard, that's all.

But he was still relatively young and still wanted to make something of himself. That was his big illusion in his thirties. He had worked part-time for the same college in New York for fifteen years and when he was certain they were about to reward him with a full-time position, they let him go. So when he was offered the job in Florida, he had to take it. He was already forty and going nowhere. He felt betrayed, felt that he had been exiled to a life of eternal boredom and mediocrity. In New York, at least, his future was never certain. Here things were much clearer, here his vision was never obscured by illusions. Here he could see the vast nothingness of his future for miles and miles ahead. The only thing he could look forward to, perhaps, along all those miles of nothingness was an occasional bowl of soup. His wife agreed to come down with him and soon she found a job teaching at the same school. It was beneath her, of course. There was little opportunity to use her vast knowledge and experience. The students were inferior to those in New York. He and his wife couldn't even get the same schedule, and whenever they did manage to see each other, they quickly made their apologies and went into different rooms to grade papers. Sometimes, when it finally seemed as if they might be able to spend some time together, his wife would invite friends over, colleagues really, and they would talk all night about all the good lessons being wasted on their students or else reminisce about foreign films they used to see in New York.

When the girl came back over to him, he immediately ordered a large soda and a two pound bag of popcorn.

"Why so much?" the girl asked.

"Because," he said. "I was hoping you'd come inside and join me."

"That's awfully nice of you," she said, "but I ain't allowed to fraternize with the customers."

She said the word "fraternize" like she wasn't quite sure what it meant, as if it had more implications than it actually did, as if it could mean anything he wanted it to mean, and this too excited him.

"Besides," she said. "I've already seen the movie a hundred times."

Then she moved her eyes up and beyond his right shoulder and he was sure the boy was behind him. He turned around slowly, but instead of seeing the boy, he saw a little man in his late fifties or early sixties with steel-framed glasses and a bow tie, and he knew that must be Mr. Johnson.

"Can we help you, sir?" Mr. Johnson asked him with that polite threatening tone movie managers often use with disagreeable patrons.

"No," he told him

"Then I suggest you get back into the theater and let this girl sell some more of that popcorn," the manager said more heartily but with an underlying tone of death and retribution.

He wanted to wring this little man's neck, but he already seemed to be in enough danger. He smiled and walked back into the theater with his large soda and giant bag of popcorn.

He knew that in no more than an hour he'd be back with the waitress again. Could it be true? The movie would end, the credits would begin to roll down the screen, the theme music would fade, the quiet and orderly march to the exits would begin, and then he'd walk just two blocks east to the restaurant where the waitress would be waiting for him. Or would she? Perhaps she had forgotten. Perhaps when he got there he'd find only the fat boy in the overalls or the tall thin boy with the broom waiting to crack his bones as if he were the chicken special on the menu.

When he got back to his seat he noticed the locale of the film had changed. It was now winter and the man and woman were freezing somewhere out in the Midwest, experiencing car trouble again and drinking something hot this time out of a thermos. Damn, he thought.

He had waited too long. Suddenly, his throat, parched from the desert, began to ache from the extreme cold. He craved soup again, but not just any soup. He was tired of the deceit he had encountered from all the roadside diners that claimed to have the best soup in the world, when all they really had was soup from a can. He was angry enough now to dump the soda and popcorn on the floor and make the tall thin boy with the broom clean it up. But instead he drank the whole cup and ate the whole bag in hopes of bloating himself so much he wouldn't have to crave soup again until he met the waitress.

By the end of the movie, the man and woman had finally fixed their car, but they split up too, the woman stealing the car and driving back to the desert, while the man walked along the cold and snowy highway sticking out his thumb and swigging down whatever soup was left in the thermos. He knew the man deserved whatever he got, always trying to pick up women along the way, including the female mechanic who fixed the car just before the woman had driven away with it.

"My engine just needed a tune-up," he had told her.

Overall, the movie had made him quite uncomfortable, and at one point he couldn't remember if it was he himself or the man in the movie who had tried to pick up the girl behind the candy counter. When the movie was officially over, when there was no chance of a new scene suddenly appearing on the screen, he sneaked out a side exit, and with his heart thumping wildly like a teenager's, he headed toward the waitress.

When he got to the restaurant she was already outside waiting for him. Unable to order anything, he didn't know what to say.

"Hi," she said, recognizing him right away. He actually thought that sitting in a dark theater all those hours would have changed his appearance somewhat.

"How was your day?" she asked.

"Fine," he told her, "but it could have used a little salt."

She laughed. "Well let's hope the soup won't," she said as he followed her home.

She had lied to him. But then again she never did claim to have homemade soup, did she? It was two in the morning and now he sat at her kitchen table while she slept in the bedroom. He had nearly died nine hours earlier when he saw her opening two cans of chicken soup for dinner. Cans—her shelves were lined with cans of soup. Did she think that a can of soup served at home made it homemade soup? What could she know about soup anyway.

He was foolish for thinking otherwise. Moments earlier, when he tried to sleep next to her, he remembered his mother's chicken soup which she had made for him all his life. But he remembered too how he hadn't always eaten it, how as a child he had often rejected her soup, complained how boring it was, although what he really meant was how time-consuming it was, how it seemed to put one long monotonous hold on the future, how it always tended to be one mindless exhausting slurp towards eternity. On the other hand, his father, as steady and constant as any other fixed object in the house, sat opposite him eating his soup with a boundless and unconscious joy which truly baffled him, which made him certain that soup was for adults, because they didn't mind sitting in one spot for a long time, because their future was behind them and they had at last settled for the long night of the soup.

"You'll be sorry one day," his mother warned him, "when you wish you had your mother's soup in front of you and it won't be there."

But he couldn't worry then about someday. Someday was way off in the future and sometimes he believed it might not exist at all.

"Maybe it just needs a little salt," she would tell him. "Maybe that's the problem."

"There is no problem," his father would answer. "It doesn't need anything. It's perfect the way it is."

But as he grew older, things changed. Just like that, he started to need the soup, looked forward to it every Friday night. Whatever it was that bothered him as a child, whatever it was about it that put his future on hold, he now welcomed as he became more uncertain of a future he could no longer control. Suddenly, he didn't want time to pass at all. He wanted things to stay the way they were. He wanted his father opposite him, relishing once again the long night of the perfect soup, and his mother who made it so hot and filled the bowls so deep that she could not help spilling some of it on her own arms as she carried it from the stove to the table. Despite the scars, for her it was a journey of love, and she never uttered a sound of pain or regret in her determination to feed her family.

Yes, he remembered how the hot soup came to him, how the steam rose before him, how like some dense fog it enveloped his father opposite him so he could hear only the long, rhythmic slurping on the other side, as of waves lapping against the shore. But when the fog lifted, there they all were, together, as one family, bound by the miracle of soup.

And then his mother would always ask, "So now you like the soup?" and he would always answer, "Of course. It just needed a little salt, that's all."

He got up from the waitress's kitchen table and opened one of the cupboards. A long line of canned soup looked out at him.

"As if I didn't know," he said to himself. She had deceived him, but it didn't matter. What did he expect anyway? What was it he was looking for? He remembered the night before he left his mother's house in Queens; his father no longer sitting opposite him at the kitchen table, he had asked her if she had made any soup, and she had said, "I'm too tired to make soup anymore. Let your wife make you soup."

He turned the lights out in the kitchen and walked towards the window. He thought he saw something outside. Had they come to get him? Had he finally, at 2:15 A.M. worn out his welcome? It was so quiet, he could hear the waitress breathing in the next room. When he lay next to her in bed, all she wanted to know was what it was like to teach, what it was like to tell people things they didn't know. Didn't he feel like a god sometimes? She would love to be a teacher but she would never know enough. She wondered whether she could absorb some of his knowledge if they slept together and made love.

"It could be like in the diner," she said. "I can be the sponge and you can be the hamburger grease."

She laughed and so did he. He liked her and wanted to tell her that nothing she believed, at least concerning him, was true. It was all a lie. Wasn't he the one who had really deceived her? Canned soup or no canned soup? He felt miserable and wanted to quit everything.

All he wanted to do now was eat soup. He appreciated what she thought, he breathed in her innocence, but still he wanted her to know it, everything, was just an illusion. But he couldn't. So he kept listening to her, and finally she asked him very softly, very gently so as not to hurt his feelings, if it would be all right if she just went to sleep. She was so tired from being on her feet all day, a real exhausting waste of time really, but what could she really do about it? She promised him they would make love in the morning because it would be a new day and she would be all refreshed.

When she fell asleep, he went into the kitchen and now he found himself looking out the kitchen window which looked over the main highway. "I'll wait to the next Campbell's truck goes by," he said to himself, "and then I'll go."

Heading home that night through the darkness, he thought about what the waitress had said. Could it be that way? Was it possible? Maybe if she could be in his class, maybe if he could look at her cornfield-yellow eyes light up when he told her things she didn't know. He was confused. He had traveled nearly two-hundred miles now and had not once stopped for soup.

One time he had seen a sign on the highway that said, "Mom's homemade chicken soup so hot and thick you might be here forever."

No, he wouldn't do it. He had been fooled for the last time. Yes, he craved his own mother's soup but knew it wouldn't be there for him any time soon. The past was gone, and he drove headlong into an uncertain future.

THE PACKAGE

He insisted I pick it up that night. I didn't want to, I was tired, but he insisted. He said if I rang his doorbell, then he'd come down and give it to me. It could have waited. One day, even two days more wouldn't have made that much of a difference. But he insisted.

So I said, "I'll come around 10. I'll ring your doorbell and then you'll come down and give it to me," I said.

"That's right," he said. "I'll come down."

"And you'll give it to me," I said.

"Yes," he said. "I'll have it in my hand. I'll give it to you and then…"

"And then what?" I suddenly asked.

"And then you'll have it," he said.

"Yes," I said. "After all, it's mine. Why shouldn't I?"

The thing was I was already quite settled. Mentally, I was in for the night. It's something you don't decide, but you know from the moment you walk in the door that you're home for good, that even before you hang up your coat, you don't think twice about whether or not you're in for the night. Then, suddenly, you're in your underwear. You look over towards your pants and they seem like they're in another country. That's the way it was when I was growing up. When my father had his pants off, we all might as well have had them off because we were all settled in for the night whether we wanted to be or not. If I tried to leave, he'd say, "Where ya goin'? Where do you think you're goin' with my pants off?"

So that's the way it was and that's the way it was for me all the way until my friend called and said, "I got it. Come over and I'll come down."

"Come down?" I asked.

"Yes, down," he said. "Into the street. And I'll give it to you."

"You could have waited until tomorrow," I told him.

"Why?" he asked. "So tomorrow you could say, 'Why don't we wait another day or two. I mean, another day or two isn't going to make that much of a difference, is it?' I mean, isn't that what you'd say," he said. "Am I right?"

He was right. But as I was saying, I felt so settled. The day was behind me already. I had already washed my face. And then there were the pants. The second my pants are off a little voice in my head says, "That's it. It's over! You, my friend are in for the night." And then this. So I called my friend back and the first thing he said was, "I knew it was you. I knew you'd call back." I told him how settled I felt.

"You know how it is," I told him. "You come in, you wash your face, you hang up your socks, you're in for the night. You know how it is."

Then there was a long silence and he said, "Did you take your pants off? Is that it?"

And I said, "Yes, that's it," and he said, after another long pause, "I was afraid of that. So do you want me to open it? Is that it? Is that what it's come down to?"

It was tempting, but it reminded me of when I was growing up and a package would come for me.

"There's a package for you," my mother would say.

"A package?" I'd ask. "For me?"

"For you," she'd say.

"For me, really?" I'd ask.

"Yes, for you," she'd say.

"Wow!" I'd say.

"Don't get so excited," she said. "We already opened it. It was nothing," she said. "The turtle was already dead."

So who wants that? If there was a package for me, shouldn't I be the one to open it? Then again, if my friend opened it, I wouldn't have to go there, at least not right away, and another dead turtle, of course, would rule it out absolutely. In fact, it was just when my friend asked me that I looked over at my socks. They were no longer on my feet but drying on the radiator. They had been in a puddle. There was no other pair in the house. They were all out, lost somewhere or at the laundry or on someone else's feet but definitely not here and the thought of putting wet ones back on was not a pleasant one. I remembered when I was growing up, my mother would show me pictures of dying children, dying because they had worn wet socks. I felt sorry for them. If they had only known my mother perhaps they would have been alive today. "If you wet your socks," she'd say, "don't bother coming home." But if I didn't come home, if I was more than a minute late from wherever it was I wasn't supposed to have gone to in the first place, I would not be allowed to leave the house at all.

I was confused. I went to ask my father what I was supposed to do, but his pants were off already, his socks were bone dry, and he was watching his favorite Western on TV. All I could hear were the sounds of gunshots and of cattle stampeding. It was **Rawhide**. My father loved **Rawhide**, but more than that he loved the theme song and more than that he loved the whipping sounds that occur twice during the song, the only two times I would see him smile all week. He said he wished he had one of those whips. "The very least life could have given me," he once told me, "was a goddamn whip." He mentioned no one in particular except Life. Life wore for my father a pair of heavy pants, and not once did it ever take them off.

When I walked in front of the TV set he said, "You don't want to live very long, do you?" My father would use dialogue from old westerns to threaten people, especially his own family. "You don't want to live very long" was his favorite, but he also had, "I'd keep my hands right where they are if I were you," or "One more step and I'll see you at the bottom of Diablo Canyon." I didn't quite get that one, but I wouldn't question it, just skulk away quietly, shaking my head up and down as if I had benefited from a piece of fatherly wisdom. All of my father's wisdom seemed to come out of his pants, though it was a bitter wisdom, born, perhaps, in suffering and destined to make us all suffer with it.

"My socks are wet," I suddenly blurted out to my friend.

But all my friend said was, "What did you do, step in a puddle?"

That got me angry, like he was going too far, so I said, "That's right, I stepped in a puddle."

"You and your wet socks," he said as if he knew something.

"Yes," I said after a long pause, "Me and my wet socks."

"Well," he said. "Do you want me to open it or not?"

"No," I said. Just like that, as if I had been rehearsing my answer for days, I said, "No, don't open it," and he said, "Fine, then I'll expect you…"

"Expect me to what?" I asked.

"Expect you to come and pick it up," he said.

"And if I did come and pick it up?" I asked him. "What then?"

"Then you'd open it," he said.

So I was back where I started. "You got three seconds to make up your mind," my friend said after another long silence.

"Three seconds?" I asked him. "What happens after three seconds?" I asked him.

"I hang up," he said. Three seconds, I thought to myself. What was it about three seconds? Then I remembered how when I was growing up everything was measured in intervals of three seconds. You have three seconds to get out of the bathroom, you have three seconds to change your clothes, to change your mind, your attitude, your girlfriend, always three seconds.

He was right. After three seconds, he hung up. I can't say I was sorry. The thing was why go anywhere when you can stay home? For God's sake, there were windows. When I was growing up, we had more windows than we knew what to do with. On Saturday mornings, we'd all wake up and head for the windows. And from any one of those windows we could see everything. There were the usual cars, the usual cement, the usual broken bottles, one old shoe lying in the middle of the street, which we could never figure out where it came from. Most of all there was old Mr. Goldblatt waiting for the mail, always waiting for the mail, his eyes glued to the corner from where like a vision the mailman would suddenly appear and though we could not see him ourselves, still from Mr. Goldblatt's eyes we could tell he was coming.

"And what's he got today, Mr. Goldblatt?" my mother would call down to him.

"Packages!" he'd yell back to her. "He's got millions of packages!"

"Really!" my mother would scream back. "I hope it's not a trick. I hope he's not trying to trick us again like last time."

That was the time the mailman said there were packages for all of us, actually started to hand them out when suddenly he started laughing, took them all back, told us he was lying, that they weren't for us at all but for some guy who never opened his door at all, who let them all pile up outside for us to stare at with terrible envy.

"Why?" I remember asking him. "Why would you do such a thing to us?" He was bored, he said. He needed a diversion.

We were all stunned. But not my father. He never believed the mailman in the first place, refused to accept even our own mail, and instead put his hands around the mailman's neck and started choking him.

"No!" we cried. "Stop! It's the mailman! You can't kill the mailman!"

I wondered perhaps if my friend just didn't want to get me out of the house, see me unsettled again, that once being unsettled, then settled, there is nothing worse than being unsettled again. That's the way it was with my socks. With all their use and re-use they had lost their elasticity, their will to live you might say. Added to all this speculation, I began to suspect there wasn't a package waiting for me at all. I'd get to my friend's house and he'd say, "Package? What package? Oh, that package? You mean the one with your name and address on it? Well, that was here, but it's not here anymore, because, well, to tell you the truth, I dumped it!"

Once when I was growing up, a package actually did arrive for us. My mother tried to open it but my father said, "I'd keep my hands right where they are if I were you." My mother ripped it open. There was a struggle. A black box fell out. Inside the black box there was another black box and then another one inside of that one and so on and so forth until they became so small we could hardly see them.

"Is this someone's idea of a joke?" my mother asked.

My father said nothing but instead began to smash each box, systematically, until there were none left, and then, and only then, removed his pants and draped them over his chair.

It was about 10:05 P.M. when I called my friend to confirm things for the last time.

"Now let me get this straight," I said to him.

"OK," he said. "Let's."

"OK," I said. "You got a package."

"That's right," he said. "A package."

I thought I heard a woman laughing in the background, laughing every time he answered me.

"And it has my name on it?"

"Yes," he said "You are…"

And he said my name and I said, "Yes, I am," and the woman laughed again and I said, "There's a woman there laughing," and he said, "There's no woman here," and then I heard her say, "What's he saying? What's going on now? Hang up! Hang up on him!"

Then he said, "Shut up!" Not to me but to her and I said, "What did you say to me?" and he said, "Not you," and I said, "So you have someone there with you," and he said, "No, there's no one else here."

"No one there besides you, you mean," I said, and he said, "No, no one at all."

"Yes, there's a woman there," I said, and he said, "There's no woman. You're hearing things. There's only me and your goddamn package and if you want it you better come and get it!"

"Or what?" I asked.

"Or…," he said.

"Or what?" I asked.

"I'll dump it," he said.

I was so agitated I started to head for my pants. But then I remembered the words I swore I'd live by after growing up with my father: Never head for your pants when you're agitated. In fact, if anything, take them off. I remembered too how my father would never hurt me when his pants were off. At those times he wasn't much use at all. You might as well have draped him over the chair with them, but when he put them on, he was unpredictable, dangerous even. There was fire in his eyes. Sometimes he'd move in my direction and then, suddenly, when he was within arms reach, close enough that if he reached out he could grab me, he'd stop. Then he'd just stare at me. I felt that if I moved a single inch, that if I pivoted my foot no more than an inch, in any direction, I might trip a wire, set off an explosive I knew only he could defuse by slowly, carefully removing his pants, first the left leg, then the right, and only then could I walk away again.

It was 10:17, only moments after I cancelled the idea of heading towards my pants, when the phone rang. I picked it up.

"It's you, isn't it?" I said.

"Yes," my friend said, "and I've been thinking."

This stunned me.

"About what?" I asked calmly. But really I was shaking, my lip was trembling, the hissing in the background had been replaced by an urgent, clanking sound as if someone was hammering his way into my apartment.

"About us," he said. "About our relationship."

"What about it?"

"It's in danger."

"Danger?"

"Yes, danger," he said. "And all because of some package…"

"Yes," I agreed. "A package."

"Yes, therefore I'm going to bring it over to you myself."

"You are?"

"Yes."

"But why?" I asked. "Why would you do that?"

"I'm bored," he said. "I need a diversion."

I was stunned. And then I thought who the hell wanted him here either? In a way it's like going out except "out" comes to you. There's that smell of "outness" when someone suddenly comes in from the outside. And, after all, he wasn't just a delivery man, was he? I couldn't just take the package and tell him to go, could I? For God's sake our friendship was in enough trouble, wasn't it? And what if he never brings a package at all? What if he says he's bringing it but never does? He's like that. Either way, I'd have to let him in. Then he'd never go. In essence, then, he himself would become the package and once opened he would spill himself all over my house, rendering himself non-returnable, un-repackageble, wetting my socks and staining my pants forever.

"Tomorrow," I said to him. "Come tomorrow."

"Why tomorrow?" he asked. "Unless you…"

"Unless what?" I asked him.

"Unless," he said. "Unless you…"

"Unless I what?" I asked.

"Never mind," he said.

"No," I said. "What were you going to say?"

"Nothing," he said.

"No," I said. "You were going to say something."

"About what?" he asked.

"About something. You said, 'unless you…' something."

"Unless you?" he asked. "Unless you what?"

"Never mind," I said.

"So I'll be right over," he said.

"That's right," I said. "You will."

After this last conversation with my friend, I nearly became paralyzed. All I could do now was to listen. I'd listen for footsteps in the street, in the hallway, out on the fire escape. Ten minutes, twenty, thirty, still no sign of him and then just as I was about to go to sleep, satisfied I was really going to be in for the night, dreaming of packages tightly wrapped, bounded by masking tape on all sides, absolutely unopenable by human hands, the doorbell rang. At first, I thought I was dreaming. I can't tell you how many times doorbells have rung in my dreams. But this one kept ringing and ringing like someone wanted to get into my dream or at least to get me out of it, until I had to admit to myself it was no dream at all but that someone was actually ringing my doorbell downstairs.

Once when I was growing up a doorbell rang in the middle of the night. All of us became paralyzed with fear.

"Who is it?" my mother asked.

No one answered.

"It's him," my father said. "He must have come."

"Who?" we asked him.

"Don't you know?" my father asked us. "Him. He's come for me."

We went for his pants. But it was too late. He had made up his mind. He pushed us away. We watched helplessly as he put them on. He looked dangerous. There was fire in his eyes and mustard stains on his pants. He unlocked the door. Then he opened it. A cold blast of air hit us from the west and he was gone.

"Maybe it was a package," my mother said. "You know how he feels about packages."

We waited all night, then days, weeks, but he never came back. Finally, my mother locked the door. The single lock, then the double lock. After this, we never got another package or letter. Our doorbell never rang again. Even old Mr. Goldblatt had disappeared from our street.

And now, again, there was the ringing in the middle of the night. I moved towards my pants but just at the point where if I extended my arm full length I could grab them off the chair, I stopped. I felt that if I moved another inch either back towards the door or forward towards the chair, I would trip some invisible wire and explode. The doorbell rang. Then it rang again. Twice more.

"It's here," I thought to myself. "It's here. It's for me."

Shots rang out. I ducked but still didn't move. I heard the sounds of cattle stampeding, men shouting, whips lashing, pots and pans crashing. Somewhere in the distance a TV was on playing my father's favorite Western.

"It's all your fault. You started this!" a voice said.

Then there was the kind of music like when there's a struggle, and another voice said, "You don't want to live very long, do you?"

The door bell rang. Another shot rang out. "I'll see you at the bottom of Diablo Canyon," a voice said. It sounded just like my father. I grabbed my pants but they did not give, as if my father himself were there pulling them away from me.

"You don't want to live, do you? You don't want to live," he kept saying that night, pushing us away, putting on his pants, running out the door. And then I remembered it was my mother who said, long after my father was gone, and only then under her breath, "It's you. It's all your fault, you started this."

The doorbell rang. The pants hadn't moved so again I went for them.

"You do want to live! You do want to live, don't you?" I cried out to them, pulling and pulling, until finally they were mine. Putting them on, I stumbled towards the radiator. The socks were dry now, dry as a bone and so hot I could hardly touch them, but despite this I put them on, despite a small voice in the back of my head that said, "Why now? There's always tomorrow isn't there?"

Despite all this, I moved towards the door, unlocked the double lock, the single lock. The door opened and a cold blast of air hit me from the west.

SIDERA

Sidera and I hadn't seen each other since '77. OK, once but that was by accident. In fact, I almost got her hit by a car that time by calling her name while she was crossing the street against the light. She often crossed against the light. She almost dared cars to hit her. She was the jaywalking champion of the world and proud of it. I was happy for her. It was her own little personal defiance against a world that was becoming too much for her. In fact, back in '77, I was one of those people. Another was her husband and then there was Jerry her boyfriend who refused to get a divorce even after she got one. Anyway, by calling her attention to me, I almost got her killed. And she had so much to live for now. Who says? She says. She says Jerry left his wife and is living with her now. The apartment as I know isn't that big but one of his cats died and one of mine and just by getting rid of the litter box I'd be surprised how much space suddenly opened up. It's not that cats take up so much space but it's that they give the appearance of doing so. They also take up a lot of air and give the impression that they will outlive you. Then, just like that, they develop some terrible infection and die. That cat, I thought, must be over a hundred years old, am I right? He was only seven, she says. Then maybe it's Jerry who's over a hundred. She laughs, but a terrible look comes into her eyes as if she suddenly remembered leaving the gas on.

Getting back to cats, one cat is like another to me and so if one dies, they all die and then of course they come back to life. This is because they have nine lives. If we all did I could be tormented by Sidera eight more times. I remembered telling Sidera back in '77 how much I loved her and how she was flattered but she was already in love with somebody else not to mention her husband and she thought the matter would end right there except I wouldn't let it despite the overwhelming odds against me. "If it weren't for Gerald and my husband," she said, "Who knows?" "Who knows?" she said to me and filled my heart with hope.

But now, right after a car's right fender has brushed against the back of her left leg, she knows. Her husband is gone, one of her cats is dead, and Jerry has moved in, and no, as it turned out she would never have loved me even if there was no one else. I didn't ask for all the information. A simple hello may have been sufficient. But no, she wanted to get things straight.

"You almost destroyed my life," she said. "But I survived." I thought for a moment she meant getting hit by the car. "I noticed," I told her. "Are you all right now?"

"Yes, now," she said. "Now I'm fine. But that does not excuse what happened before." I agreed with her.

The next time I met her was three years later. I didn't actually meet her face to face but rather unexpectedly by phone.

"And another thing…" she said. I still hadn't quite recognized her voice. "Harassing me at that particular time of my life not to say any time is all right although you being a man might think so while having all that trouble with Jerry and my husband was unforgivable."

"Sidera?" I asked.

"You have to learn like all men that you just can't impose you feelings on someone just because you happen to have them at the moment."

"This is you, Sidera, isn't it?" I asked

"I just hope you've grown up a little. I really do," she added.

"I'm doing my best," I told her. "I really am. But tell me. Who is this?"

"You know damn well who this is," she said. "Apparently you still feel you have to try and get my attention any way you can, don't you?"

"Wait a minute," I said. "Who called whom?"

You see I hadn't called her for seven years and that's in comparison to having called her at least twice a day for two years starting back in '77. One night I chased a taxi for over three blocks in Chinatown because I thought she might be in it. "Come back, Sidera! Come back!" I cried. "You know I didn't mean it." That was funny. There were so many beautiful Chinese women standing around watching me in that mysterious way but all I could think of was Sidera. It seemed to be the Chinese New Year. Anyway, there was something festive going on but I wasn't in the mood. Huge dragon heads blocked my way at every corner but all I could see was Sidera's face. There were loud explosions everywhere, things appeared too close and I could actually see the creases in the black pants of those who brought up the dragon's rear. I was in a vortex of mad Chinese revelry and I couldn't get out. I felt trapped, as if I should have gotten out of here before. But for some reason forgot to. I know the reason. I was in love. I felt that everything going on out there, the lights, the noise, the swirling of the dragon's tail, merely reflected what was going on in my own heart, and before I knew it there I was with the others beneath the dragon's clothes zig-zagging though the crooked streets. It was funny. I thought now of Sidera sitting quietly in the back of a taxi while I, part dragon, moved blindly through the bowels of some deep dark celebration. Where was all this leading to? I wondered if I could get the others to cooperate and steer this thing back to Queens just to let her see what she had done to me, how she had at last driven me into frenzy.

Frenzy or not the next thing I know is I'm standing in front of her door at three in the morning with a piece of dragon hanging from my lips, crying for forgiveness, and smelling like a Roman candle. She ran downstairs to shut me up. "Are you out of your mind?" she asked." "It's three o'clock in the morning!"

That was one time but there were times I just called her on the phone to tell her that whenever I thought about her my heart flinched. She didn't care. She didn't know what I was talking about. I was being abstract, romantic. I told her that I wouldn't bother her anymore if she could explain why whenever I thought about her my heart flinched. She said I had to work that out for myself. "Go to a cardiologist," she said. "Maybe it's just a murmur and you're blaming it on the wrong thing. Maybe you can but I can't afford to be romantic anymore. It's more trouble than it's worth." For someone who pined for another woman's husband she certainly could be cold and practical about someone else's pining. I needed compassion and my heart flinched for a woman who wouldn't give it to me. She thought I was harassing her. Sometimes her about-to-depart husband would answer the phone and I'd have to hang up. Other times her about-to-return boyfriend would answer the phone and I'd have to hang up. Who was harassing whom? This double-headed monster—the husband and the boyfriend—eating up her life was digging its claws into mine as well.

What does she know about romance? Does she have any idea how I even got back from Chinatown? About the rival dragon that suddenly came steaming down the opposite street, bullets shooting out of its nostrils, our own head riddled to pieces, how, even in my drunken stupor, I knew enough to play dead and when the coast was clear roll out from under the dragon lifeless skin, jump into a cab and play with the driver's ears until he threatened to toss me off the Queensboro bridge? I doubt it. It took some eyewitness news report to remind me about the next evening. I wished to God she could have seen me crawling out of that dragon but now I understand how little difference that would have made. Dragon, shmagon, that's not real life, she would say. Real life is not getting drunk and running away but it is seriously confronting one's own innermost being which will then hopefully result in one copulating with the right person.

"I just wanted to let you know," she said from the other end of the phone, "that no thanks to you things are working out so much better for me now. I'm starting to clear up a lot of things in my life." I was genuinely glad to hear it even if things were still pretty muddled in mine. After she hung up, I tried to think whether I should think of this as anymore than what it was, which in itself may have been more than it appeared to be or whatever it was it was unusual to say the least, but then I remembered how seven years earlier Sidera had answered one of my nagging love letters by insisting that she shouldn't even have given me the satisfaction of reading it let alone answering it because I would inevitably misinterpret this act as showing some kind of interest in me, which sick and demented response she would never put past me. On the contrary she wished to shatter all hope, to cut the string that flinched my heart and then she signed the letter "Sincerely yours," a final and inexorable slap in the face. So now, over seven years later, far more stable and mature, far less sick and demented, I would not jump to any false conclusions. But even so couldn't this sudden phone call, coming after such a long interval, indicate a desire, if not unconscious to rekindle my hopes, to get my heart flinched again? Look, it doesn't flinch for anyone and maybe now Sidera was mature enough to realize that. And maybe her boyfriend left her for good this time and now instead of three guys vying for her love there were none. And as for me still carrying a torch for her after all these years? Well, that too she would never put past me.

Two days later, in the middle of a baseball game in which my team is losing 3-2 in the ninth, two outs, nobody on base and my favorite player up representing the tying run at the plate, she calls again. The phone rings and I cry, "Shit! They're doing it to me again," "they" being anyone who didn't watch baseball and "it" being depriving me of one of the few pleasures left to me since my heart stopped flinching some 7-9 years ago. So I let the phone ring awhile, defiance I guess, while my favorite player, let's call him Willie, keeps fouling it off with two strikes on him, and when I finally pick up the phone, Willie strikes out to end the game. "Hello?" I ask.

"And another thing…" she says. "Don't get any ideas because I'm calling you like this that it means anything. I'm just doing what my shrink told me to do which is to confront all my old ghosts, all those that made my life miserable and then to just get it all behind me so that I can finally get on with my life. Do you understand?" I told her yes, but all I really understood at that moment was that Willie struck out.

"Good," she said. "Because the last thing I want you to do is to get the wrong idea. Right now Jerry is about the best thing that ever happened to me and I don't want anything or anyone spoiling that including you." I could hear the crowd booing Willie. I felt bad for him and turned the TV off. I wondered whether if I didn't turn it on again for nine years they'd still be booing.

"Don't worry," I told her. "My heart doesn't flinch anymore."

"Are you sure?" she asked.

"Last time I checked," I told her.

"Then just keep it that way," she warned.

After she hung up, I turned the TV back on. Willie was being interviewed in the post-game show. He was explaining about the pitch he struck out on. "I just missed it," he said. "I knew it was coming but I just missed it. No excuses." It seemed so simple. Just one pitch, that's all and he happened to miss it. There would be thousands of more pitches for Willie to swing at before it was all over, I thought. It wasn't the end of the world. Life was full of chances. You had to see and then catch them that's all.

One time, right before Sidera signed her letter "Sincerely yours," my heart flinched. Then it didn't anymore but just went back to pumping blood through my body like it always did, as if I didn't care anymore. That was nine years ago. How can someone even pretend to hope anymore after nine years.

Then, later that night, she called again.

"And another thing…" she said.

"What's that?" I asked.

"I moved," she said.

"Where?" I asked.

"Wouldn't you just like to know," she said

Moved? I couldn't believe it. The cat dying, one less litter box, the boyfriend dumping all his stuff there, and now moving? No. she knew that was the one thing I couldn't believe. Not seeing her for nine years was one thing but not knowing where she was anymore? Not being able to pass by her apartment anymore just on the chance of catching a glimpse of her? No, hope may come to an end but there is a limit to its finality. Something was up. I ran to her apartment. Her name was still there. She was lying. Ring it, I thought. Ring it. So I rang it. I just kept my finger on it for hours and then suddenly, almost unbelievably, it rang back. She was letting me in! Perhaps it was all a mistake. Perhaps she was expecting someone else. It kept ringing. Perhaps it would never ring again. I thought about Willie getting one of those fat fastballs just asking to be crushed and I knew he wouldn't miss it this time. I pushed open the door. My heart flinched again and I went with it.

THE CRULLER

I had a date but I was much too early. There was a coffee shop across the street where I could sit at a counter and have a cup of coffee.

"Cup of coffee," I told the waitress. She made a face like what else is new in this boring, fucking world and then poured me the coffee, piping hot, so black you could dive in and never be seen again. I hated to spoil it with milk except I couldn't stand it black. The milk wasn't sour from smelling it but it didn't stop looking bad from the moment I poured it and then it wouldn't dissolve, and then only reluctantly.

I missed the waitress. Already I missed the waitress. No sooner do I meet someone and I already miss them. When she came by to switch ketchup bottles, I smiled at her, so she asked me what I wanted. "Nothing," I said.

I lied. I wanted her. She told me I was wrong if I thought the cruller under the glass bowl was stale. It may look old and filthy, she said, but it was still pretty fresh, fresh despite everything, despite the passing of two weeks, despite people poking their noses into it. Not even the radiation every one was worried about would get through. In all honesty, all kidding aside, it was true. It was still fresh.

How it could be? I wondered. The waitress had to be lying. I would never know. I thought about my date. Should I take her here? I wonder if she'd lie to her, being a woman and all. What was on the menu? If they had meatloaf, I was home free. Girls liked meatloaf. This was my experience.

"How's the meatloaf," I asked.

"We ain't got meatloaf," she said.

So much for the meatloaf, I thought, keeping a close watch on the time. I thought my minute hand was stuck. If only three minutes went by, then what was to stop twenty minutes from having gone by, or thirty, or a thousand? My date may already think I'm not coming. I pictured her ordering pizza and then digging into it with huge bites.

I wondered what the waitress was doing tonight. Me and the waitress. The waitress and I. In my mind I repeated certain key phrases such as "When do you get off?" and "So, When do you get off?" and "Do you ever get off?" and then realized how far away from that I was, like being adrift at sea and suddenly waking to find myself far from shore. There was a vast empty universe between thinking and saying it.

She looked quite good in her blue uniform. Here was instinct. Me and the waitress. The waitress and I. Alone in the house of instinct. We wouldn't talk about poetry and if she wanted to I'd discourage all thought. We'd go back to her apartment. She would not be living with her mother but in some apartment some guy had walked out on her in. I'd say how clean it was and she'd get defensive and say, "Whaddya expect, a pig sty? Just because I work in a dump don't mean I gotta live in one too. I bet you think I'm stupid too, so that's why you don't wanna talk about poetry. Well, fuck you!"

Then I'd watch her struggle in and out of that uniform day and night, twice a day, this great burden; this something, but I'd watch her with a cold observer's eye and believe it represented something, something great, some greater struggle, her life, my life, our lives, and then I'd be sure to write about it one day. I'd always recall the struggle. Who the hell asked you to? She'd probably say. And then I'd recall the great sex, simple, honest, pure, multifaceted, frequent and disgusting to the cold observer's eye.

My mind was back at the counter again. It had risen from its dreams like the steam out of the coffee and settled on the ceiling.

Where was she? Back in the kitchen, no doubt, to be harassed, molested, vulgarized. Each time she reappears she's like an actress leaving the real-life pressures backstage, behind her, and each time a bit more broken and worn down.

On the other hand, experience gives so much raw depth to her performance. I'd never recognize her without the uniform. Her whole essence is packed inside it. That is everything she is to me.

"Would you like some more coffee?" she asks with the same reluctance the milk had to dissolve.

"No thanks. This is fine," I say. It is.

"If you say so," she said, slapping the bill down on the counter and knocking over some left-over glass filled with ice. The ice spilled in my direction but fell just short of the table's edge.

"Did it get on you?" she asked indifferently, almost as if she were asking whether I wanted the peas or the string beans.

"No," I said. "And it was only ice, not coffee or anything."

"That was yesterday," she said, "except yesterday I didn't miss."

We both laughed. I noticed the joyful glimmer of her yellow teeth. I felt a sudden rush of excitement in my bowels like right before a big game.

"Do I pay you?" I asked with a new confidence I would save for my date.

"The cashier," she said, pointing at a man chomping at a cigar behind the cash register just to the left of where I first walked in, and there was some guy paying his bill as if by example and I could hear the cigar-chomper telling him to go fuck himself.

"Why don't you just go fuck yourself," he said with that kind of cigar-chomping confidence and matter of fact pleasure he was made for at moments like this.

"Why don't you do yourself a favor and go fuck yourself."

"Oh yeah?" the customer replied. "Well I just hope that one day you'll have to eat your own food and then see how you like it!"

"Drop dead," countered the man with the cigar.

"Your mother!" shouted back the customer, smashing his fist on the counter and sending up a little ring from the register.

"Your mother!" The man behind the counter didn't flinch.

"Get the hell out of here or I'll call a cop," he threatened without any kind of anger or hysteria but with that same matter-of-factness which made it all the more threatening.

"Go ahead and call one!" retorted the dissatisfied customer, but rather half-heartedly, already making a move toward the door.

"It's not me he'll arrest for trying to poison someone with that soup. No sir, not me!"

The cashier looked at him like a boxer who's got his man on the ropes, and then said so all the street could hear,

"And don't come back or it'll be your balls in the soup next time!"

This last comment stunned me more than anything else. It was the kind of comment one makes when confidence quickens the imagination. The waitress laughed, but it was not the laugh of someone enjoying the cruel fate of another but only the laugh of someone transposed temporarily into a world of pure joy.

"Charlie, you're a panic!" she cried out to the man behind the register. "How in the world do you think of such things? How do you do it? You're a genius, a poet! Damn, I love you, Charlie. How the hell would I ever get by without you? Damn it, Charlie, there's no one like you in the whole world. Nobody!"

"Thanks, Janine," Charlie said. "But nobody's gonna put down our food. Nobody!"

"Nobody, Charlie," she said. "We got the best stuff in the world and nobody's gonna put it down while I'm still around. No sir!"

"You said it, baby!" he told her. "Love it or leave it!"

"Some nerve that guy had, hunh, Charlie?" she asked.

"Some nerve!" he answered, and then he winked at her and I knew he had it. From where I sat he had it all under control. The money, the customers, the women; they were his. With the flick of an ash he controlled the universe. It was a perfect world and he controlled it all from behind that cash register. He would never even have to come out. God help the customer who would ever make him come out from behind that cash register. It wouldn't be me. I didn't even want him to have to make change. I searched my pockets for the exact change. I found it and considered myself very lucky.

It was going to be a good night. I went up to pay my bill and he asked how everything was. I looked back at Janine and she had a terrible look as if she had failed me somehow, failed all of us.

"He wouldn't eat the cruller, Charlie," she said. "I couldn't sell it for nothin'." For the first time all night I felt threatened. I thought they might even make me eat the soup.

"I wasn't very hungry," I said. "But I would like to come back and have it someday. I really would. It wasn't her fault. It's that I have this date and…but the coffee was terrific, just terrific!"

"Glad you liked it!" exclaimed Charlie, never intending me any harm. "We aim to please."

"Next time," I swore to him. "Next time the cruller."

"That's okay," he said. "If not you, someone else. We always get our man."

"Or woman," added Janine.

Charlie said nothing. He had said it all. I looked at the cruller and I noticed that Janine too was looking at it with a terrible nostalgia I would never understand, and her face looked as if she were thinking about putting that uniform on and taking it off again, every day, twice a day, and I knew her struggle was not just a dream. And I knew then that the cruller would never be sold. It would sit there for all eternity while Janine tried to sell it and Charlie promised it would be sold. Charlie would always be there to offer hope and sometimes joy and Janine was there to receive it and no doubt neither wanted the cruller sold. As long as it sat under its glass bowl (and the longer it sat there the longer it would sit there), Janine would stand behind it and Charlie up front behind the register, always offering hope and sometimes joy and controlling this world with absolute control and confidence like a god. Everything would be okay. It was old and stale and no one in their right mind would ever eat it. That's what it would take, all right, I thought, someone not quite in their right mind to upset the balance of this little universe.

So I said good-bye to Charlie and he said to come again and I said again I'd have the cruller next time and he laughed and said I'd better or he'd make me eat the soup with that guy's balls in it and I could hear Janine laughing as I headed into the street, full of confidence and joy, knowing my date would be waiting, and I heard her say,

"You're a panic, Charlie, a real panic," so this is how people get happy, I thought.

THE KEY CHAIN

The first thing I did when I woke up was to take out my baseball glove from the hall closet. I had just woken from one of those early evening naps I started taking ever since I started seeing Christine. When I got out the glove, I noticed immediately how stiff it was and it gave me a bad feeling thinking about all those balls that popped out if it last summer. There was no telling how next summer would be; after all, it was still January, but nevertheless I suddenly felt like getting a big jump on things, so I decided to oil it now. But before I could even get the rag out, the phone rang and as suddenly and unexpectedly as that feeling of getting the advantage over something had come, so had it left.

The phone rang and it was Christine, who wanted to know if I had opened the gift yet which she had left for me on the night table next to the bed. I almost forgot Christine. I don't really connect my naps to whomever or whatever causes me to take them so I had genuinely forgotten Christine. It's not necessarily that I didn't love her; although with Christine love is a funny word to use. Actually, it's that I really didn't know whether I loved her or not. She never really gave me a chance to think about it. If I said I did, then she said I didn't and if I said I didn't, then she said I really did except I was afraid to admit it to myself. "You know you love me," she would say. "Who doesn't?" That kind of generalizing about our relationship bothered me so I decided that when she was gone she didn't exist and when she was here no one existed but her. After all it was the uncertainty I couldn't live with so I thought this might be a good compromise.

I put down the receiver and raced into the bedroom. Yes, it was there. A small gift. A baseball key chain.

"What's this supposed to mean?" I asked her.

"Why does everything always have to mean something?" she asked. "Why not just accept it as a gift pure and simple from me to you? Does everything I do have to mean something?" Perhaps she was right, but then again, why should I believe her? How many other men were waking from naps right at this moment finding little gifts she had left for them on the night table? Christine cheated. No question about it. Why else would she suddenly get up in the middle of the night and leave my house? Because she was heading straight for someone else's bed, that's why. We were done anyway. No use wasting valuable time. There were bartenders heading home right now pumped for action while I was already quite spent. To be honest it made sense. That is, it looked good on paper. But what about the intangibles? What about feelings? Didn't she think I had any feelings? Is this what made me take out my baseball glove? What made me think I could ever stop balls from popping out of it just by oiling it? I might as well oil my bed to prevent Christine from popping out of it at night.

"So what did you get the others?" I asked her.

"What others?"

"Your others. The graveyard shift."

"I don't know what you're talking about."

"Oh, come on."

"You don't know."

"Then why always leave in the middle of the night?"

"We were finished anyway. What's the difference?"

"I don't like cheating."

"Who's cheating? And even if I was cheating, what makes it cheating? And what makes you think it would be you I was cheating on?"

I couldn't follow this exactly but it sounded like one of her typical evasions.

"Then are we together or no?" I asked her.

"Of course we are," she said. "When I'm there we're together, when I'm not there we're not. That's all. Just try to work that out and don't get crazy."

But I couldn't work it out. It was too crazy. I needed to be sure of things.

"The gift is very nice," I told her. "You shouldn't have."

"I almost didn't. But then I thought what the hell. Anyway, it sucks. The last thing you need is a key chain. But that's not the point."

"What is?" I asked, still not quite following this.

"The point is...the point is...to read it."

At this point the operator came on requesting another five cents. Every time she called me was from a different phone booth. The girl had no consistency and I played right into her hands.

"How many goddamn nickels does she think I have?" she complained. Was this a slip of the tongue? To my thinking this was only our first interruption. "Better take down the number."

She knew I couldn't protest. How could I with the operator bearing down on us, threatening to cut us off any second. The pressure was too much and so I went with my instincts. Stay with her, they said. Wait this thing out. So once again, I wrote down one of her filthy little phone numbers and once again I felt indifferent and alone, dirty and unloved, disconnected from a world of warm and familiar numbers, numbers from which strong relationships can be built. And after I had written it down, I looked at it and for the life of me I could not recognize my own sick and desperate scrawl. Why, I thought, I might as well be one of the horrible callers who frequent these phone booths all the time, one of those deceased and desperate creeps who get their kicks out of being anonymous. There was something wrong with me giving in to her like this. But before calling her back, I read the message on the little baseball part of the key chain: "Property of Petie Kress." Petie Kress was the little boy who had been missing for two years, last seen playing baseball with his little friends in the park. I picked up the phone and dialed. It rang three times before she answered. "What took you so long?" I asked.

"Some guy was trying to use the phone." Some guy this and some guy that. Why was it always some guy? Why couldn't it be some blue-haired lady sometime muscling her way into the phone booth?

"What guy?" I asked.

"Would you know if I told you? Some guy. That's all."

"So?"

"So I told him I was expecting a call."

"Who from?"

"From you asshole."

"So how'd you talk him out of it?"

"I shot him"

"You did?"

"What the hell's wrong with you? Of course I didn't shoot him. Who even has a gun? You gotta loosen up. You're too uptight. You really are."

"I know. I was just curious. That's all."

"Just relax. I'm here aren't I?" This always bothered me. This "I'm here aren't I" business always gnawed at me.

"You're hiding something," I told her.

"What could I be hiding? I'm in a phone booth, for godsakes!"

"Yes, but you have a way," I said

"A way of what?"

"A way. That's all. A way." She did have a way. I was never able to describe it very well, but she did have a way.

"Just tell me what you thought of the message and then I'm gonna hang up."

"It was very nice. It was a very nice sentiment. I'm sure if anyone found it I'd be arrested for kidnapping."

"What are you so pissed about now?" she asked.

"Nothing," I said. "Are you coming…" That's when we were cut off. There was only silence. When I spoke I heard my own voice come back to me. "Christine," I cried. "What the hell is going on here!?" Then I could hear the line open again. I could hear street sounds, sirens, the honking of cars, men and women screaming.

The operator asked for another five cents. "Christine," I said. "Are you there?"

My ear was alone against the night. I had no choice but to listen to whatever was out there. Why was she doing this to me? I couldn't make any sense out of any of it. I was alone and helpless inside a night where nothing seemed to be going right, which seemed to be bursting at its seams. I could only think that she let the receiver drop and then went for a walk. I hated this. How could she drop my ear like this into that terrible void of uncertainty? Who knows what's out there, what could suddenly seize this phone and speak into my ear? The shouting got louder. There seemed to be a fight going on. It was difficult to construct a real picture in my mind, but somehow I could sense that the phone wire was swinging wildly and just sensing this made me dizzy.

All I had was my ears and that was a dreadful position to be in. I felt that if just someone could explain to me what was going on, I would be quite calm and far less dizzy. I yearned to be put on hold. I wanted to be shielded from those terrible and uncertain sounds of life going wrong and listen to soothing elevator music instead. But there was something she wanted me to hear, to make sense of, to learn from and then to apply in a mature way to my understanding of our relationship and relationships in general. The hell with it, I thought. She'll just have to call back. But just as I was about to hang up, the screaming got louder and then more familiar.

It was her. "Christine," I cried once again. "Are you all right?"

"Yes," she cried back. "It was just some jerk trying to strangle me."

"Oh," I said. "I thought you hung up on me."

"I'm serious," she said. "Some jerk just pulled me out of the booth and tried to strangle me."

"Do you mean 'strangle'?" I asked. "Or do you mean 'strangle' in the sense of someone tapping you a bit too high on the shoulder?"

"What do you call some guy ripping his fingernails into my neck and cutting off my oxygen supply?" she asked.

"Where is he now?" I asked. "And did you get his phone number?"

"What's the matter?" she asked. "You don't believe me?"

"I believe you," I said. "Only it seems so unbelievable."

"You just can't deal with surprises." She said.

"I guess you're right."

She was right. To deal with her I always had to deal with uncertainties and surprises.

"Uncertainty is what it's all about," she'd say. "Surprise! What's life without surprises? Like what a great surprise it would be if they found that kid. It would have almost been worth losing him!"

So I supposed if I wanted to continue seeing her, I'd have to get used to her springing out of my bed at three in the morning or getting strangled in phone booths.

"Is there something you'd like me to do?" I asked her.

"No," she said. "Gotta go now. Bye." And she was gone.

I waited five, maybe ten minutes, but she didn't call back. I tried to recall the phone number by memory but couldn't and so felt somewhat relieved I was still my own man. But what was I to do now? Was I supposed to work this out too? Had she really been strangled or was this just another attempt to keep me off guard, to force me to continually expect the unexpected? In a few hours she came in sporting a neck brace.

"Have an accident?" I asked.

"Right," she said. "Just be happy I'm alive."

I suppose I was happy about that. But I wondered whether I was more happy than the others were. Was this a test? Was she gauging our reactions and choosing the best one?

"Yes," I said. "I'm glad you're still alive. In fact I bought an extra orange soda to celebrate."

"You're the best," she said.

"I am?" My heart leaped.

"Don't go nuts," she warned. "It's just an expression."

"Does it hurt?" I asked, wishing to change the subject.

"Of course it does. Why do you ask?"

"No reason," I told her. "Just checking."

"Checking what? If it really happened?"

"No. Not exactly. It's just that I can't believe you were being strangled while talking to me on the phone."

"Well, believe it."

"And then you came straight to me."

"I don't go straight to anyone."

"But I was the first."

"Of course."

"Or was I?"

"Are you starting that again."

"It's been five hours."

"I went to the emergency clinic. Five hours is nothing for the emergency clinic."

"Then you came to me first."

"Who else was I gonna come to?"

"You tell me."

"Don't get crazy."

"I would just like to know. Just for the hell of it."

"Just loosen up, will ya? If you could just learn to loosen up things would be great between us."

"I don't want to loosen up."

"You mean you don't know how."

"Have all the others loosened up yet?"

"Just give me the orange soda," she demanded.

I watched her drink the orange soda. Her neck still looked strong but her face had a pained expression on it.

"How was it?" I asked.

"Great."

"You looked like you were in pain."

"No, I was just faking it."

I just couldn't loosen up. I needed answers. Answers, one way or another would help me loosen up. Even if she had her own phone number would help me loosen up. I wanted her to come right out and say no I wasn't strangled. I staged it all to see how much you really care about me. I am ready now to drop the bartenders. The casual creepers among strange phone booths, the stray college professor, and to settle down with you. Yes, I have now some very specific and definite goals and I want to achieve them with you.

"You've got the look again," she said.

"What look," I asked.

"The impossible one." And what if she did stay. If she did only love me? It wouldn't be her anymore. Or maybe it would be her until three in the morning and then someone else. Let's take this latest strangling for example, imaginary or otherwise. Some guy is out there minding his own business. But then he passes by the phone booth and spots her. She's got the post-three-o'clock-in-the-morning look, something about those eyes, don't ask what it is, I can't explain it, I quite haven't had it that bad yet, not bad enough to strangle her. Anyway, unlike the old man in the Poe story, at least she keeps them closed at night. That's something. Otherwise, they're always wide open; they hardly ever blink unless she wills it, and most of all, they do not reflect but consume light. This consuming of light has something to do with the natural human urge to strangle her. It makes people uncomfortable. It causes too many complications in any give and take relationship. So the guy, who normally reflects the warm glow of domesticity, spots her and starts to get sucked in. But he does not want to spend eternity cowed in darkness just beneath her right eyelid, to be whipped and lashed whenever it suited her to blink. So to avoid complications, to avoid uncertainty, he tries to strangle her, and quickly, so he could get home for dinner on time. Yes, I understand now. With her you can have it no other way. You must loosen up or else.

"Are you really worried about me?" she said.

"Of course," I said watching out for that eye.

"You love me, don't you?"

"Yes."

"And I'm not cheating on you, right?"

"Right."

"And I'll always be here for you, right?"

"Right."

And at three in the morning she was gone. But the key chain was still there. Someday I might even put some keys on it. But not yet. "Property of Petie Kress." Wouldn't it be something if he came back one day, I thought.

THE CAT

There was no intercom, just a buzzer, so I let them in. They came right up to my door, knocked on it, and when I asked who it was they said, "Us." That was good enough for me. When they walked in, I thought I recognized one of them, the one with the tangled hair and the thick red eyes like tomato juice. Maybe it's from college that I knew him, I thought.

"We don't what nothin'," tangled hair said, eying the TV set, the stereo, the VCR, the CD and the DVD player.

The other guy, the one whose face looked like a badly torn envelope, said nothing. "How's life?" I asked them as if we had been friends for years and in a way I wanted that, I wanted them to think I cared, that I had no evil intentions towards them.

"Just great," tangled hair said. "Got anything to drink?"

I handed him my last bottle of scotch. I figured it would make them feel at home since I had always noticed the homeless drinking scotch in my hallway.

Then envelope face looked at me and said, "Are those your real teeth?" I laughed, but he was serious and when he reached out to touch them with his fingers, I shut down my mouth real hard like the lid of a piano. Then I started to smell them. They really smelled badly and this more than anything reminded me of college and the old days of not showering and wearing torn, dirty clothes. Tangled hair drank his scotch from the bottle like it was lemonade on a hot day and even envelope face shook his head in amazement and when he did things flew out of his hair, some dead some alive. Then envelope face went to work. He grabbed the scotch from tangled hair, swigged down the rest of it, and then wiped his mouth with his sleeve like in the old westerns. Then he took out his knife, brandished it around the apartment for a while and said, "Now what do you got around here that I can cut up?"

I thought about the cat. I forgot all about the cat my neighbor left here for the weekend so he could go upstate and visit his girlfriend. Then I thought about all those girlfriends that for some reason or other live upstate and how now a cat was going to die for it.

"Put that damn thing away," tangled hair told him.

At last, I thought, a voice of reason.

"There's plenty of time for that later," he went on. "We've got to get some pussy first."

He really seemed determined to stick to a schedule. This gave me some time to excuse myself to go to the bathroom. They might have stopped me, but they seemed to like the idea there was a bathroom, so I exhorted them to make themselves at home and went looking for the cat. In the bathroom I noticed the cat was right where I expected it to be, right in the litter box. The cat tried to get away, so I grabbed it and tied a note around its neck. I had a note for every occasion for life in the big city. This one said, "Help, I am being tortured in my own apartment. Please send help. Sincerely, Weinstein, 4A."

But then, suddenly, all the cat wanted to do was play. It licked my face and then rubbed its cheek against it. It looked into my eyes and I became totally consumed by it. Perhaps I would speak to my neighbor about this when he came back. My neighbor was grossly misinformed about cats. Cats do not sit on window sills looking out at cars blurring by but study human beings in action in order to determine whether or not they were worth being saved. I think they're already getting tired of us, of that superior "you'll eat when I'm ready to feed you," attitude and it's just a matter of time before they abandon us completely. I tremble when I come upon a cat in some deserted alley and it simply walks by me, not once stopping to stare into the deepest core of my soul. And now, fighting off that special attraction between us, I tossed it out the bathroom window and watched it spread its legs and land right on top of one of the great garbage heaps of the city. I had seen him do this so many times with my neighbor who loves the cat but who I think would much rather have a bird.

From the bathroom, I could hear chirping noises, as if small birds had alighted upon the window sills. When I came out, I saw tangled hair and envelope face smacking their lips at the whores in the street. When I joined them at the window, I noticed one looking up and around, confused, not knowing where the sounds were coming from. Her arms went out, her palms upward as if pleading for more clues to our whereabouts. Taxis stopped for her but she kicked their doors and spat at their tail pipes as they sped down the street.

"Fourth floor!" tangled hair yelled out.

I was worried. What if the neighbors heard?

I buzzed in the whore without asking. The funny thing is she really did look familiar. The first thing I thought of was college; in fact, I wracked my brain going over every class I ever took but still I couldn't place her. The boys looked at her like they were starving and she was the Chinese food.

"Would you like to wash up?" I asked the woman.

"Why?" she asked. "Do I look dirty? Do I smell? You should have thought of that before you buzzed me in and made me burst my lungs walking up here. My job is a lateral one. It is not straight on, it is not up and down, it is lateral."

She seemed to enjoy using that word, and it seemed to turn the boys on too.

"That's just what we're looking for," said tangled hair. "Some lateral action."

But envelope face disagreed.

"Up and down!" he said. "I just want the old up and down!"

The woman laughed but only like when you see a couple of zoo animals pretending to be what they're not and fumbling around badly in their cage.

"Two hundred bucks up front," she said, "and you boys can go in any direction you want."

The boys laughed very hard.

"Since when you been workin' on Park Ave.?" tangled hair asked.

"Since I took a look at you two," she said. "And who are you?" she asked looking at me. "Our host?"

"With the most," tangled hair said sweeping his arms across the room of TVs, VCRs, CDs, DVDs like he was Vanna White showing off prizes on Wheel of Fortune.

"I think I'm the victim," I told her, looking at the boys, hoping they'd laugh, but they just looked at me like they were deciding whether to just throw me in with everything else or toss me into the garbage. I was beginning to feel unwanted and knew I'd have to stand there now with some kind of decisive expression or other. But I think it was too late and I thought if this was a movie we'd be just up to the part where the squeamish start to cover their eyes and everyone else gets ready for the blood and gore.

"Do I know you from somewhere?" I asked the woman. "You look very familiar."

"No wonder," she said. "I'm usually standing right outside your front door or else lurking in the hallways if someone buzzes me in."

"Not that," I said. "Way back. Years ago. Like in college."

The boys laughed, but you could see they were impatient.

"Yeah, we all knew each other from college," tangled hair said. "We used to be in the fraternity together."

But the woman didn't flinch. She had this look on her face now like she had been caught doing something bad and started to close up her jacket to hide her breasts more. Tangled hair and envelope face just wanted to get started, so they tugged on the woman's arm but she just kept pulling away from them looking at me the whole time.

"Yeah, sure," I said. "Don't you remember? Mr. Bloom's English class. That's where I met you. English 105: History of English Literature."

"Yeah, sure," she said laughing. "The History of the English Fucken Language!"

"Fuck!" tangled hair said, grabbing her right arm.

"Shit!" envelope said grabbing her left arm.

As for me, I wish we could have gotten past this whoring crap and brewed up a nice cup of coffee and just talked about old times.

But the boys would never stand for it. I knew that the minute they dragged her over to the couch, and at the moment I wondered what Mr. Bloom would have thought about all this, good old Mr. Bloom who kept telling us how much potential we had to be great in the world and how it was our responsibility to make the world a better place to live in and how you had to start with an appreciation of good literature and a solid foundation of grammar because the power of the English language was the greatest power on earth and so forth and so on and I looked at tangled hair and envelope face just giving it to her like that while I stood there helpless, although with a solid foundation of grammar behind me so first I tried the imperative and said, "Stop it or I'll…!" and then the conditional and said, "If you don't stop, I'll…!" and finally the subjunctive saying, "If I were you I wouldn't…!" but nothing helped and then I looked towards the open window and there stood my neighbor's cat just staring at the woman with the boys on her.

At first I wondered what it was doing there, the note still tied around its neck and then I remembered that cats do not use buzzers. "Attack!" I wanted to say but I knew that if the cat did anything at all it would only be because it had determined through careful study that the woman, myself, even the boys were worth saving. So there I stood, helpless in the middle of my living room, in the middle of a world of reckless indecision, waiting for the cat to make up its mind.

ALASKA

She assumed she had been named Alaska because she was born there. She never questioned it. Not even once. Then, just like that, her parents died. Now she wanted to know, now that it was too late. No one else knew. She had an aunt named Virginia but that was pretty normal, not enough to assume that there was any pattern there, any real family inclination to name children after states.

I loved her the moment I saw her. She said her name was Al and I assumed it was short for Alice or something like that so I never questioned it either until I noticed an application of some sort she had to fill out sitting on the kitchen table that required the applicant's full name. I looked at it more than once assuming she had mistakenly put her place of birth where the name should be.

"They all think that," she told me. "Or else they reject the application thinking it's some kind of joke which it probably is."

She was obviously down on herself. She grew depressed. She felt alienated, not a part of the main. I asked her why she didn't ask her parents why they named her Alaska. She said she didn't want to embarrass them.

"It could have been some irreparable mistake," she said. "It could have been an irreparable mistake that they felt compelled not to rectify. When my mother got pregnant again I got angry and said, 'If it's a boy will you call him Hawaii?' And then there was this deadly pall over the room. No one said a word only my mother screamed and grabbed her belly as if I meant to harm it, as if I meant to get even with them for giving me that name. So I never said another word about it and I never told anyone my real name, not even you until you saw it on that application though I suppose I left it there purposely unconsciously so you'd find it."

I asked her why she didn't change it. Just go down to city hall or wherever one goes and change it but she wouldn't because she felt she would be betraying her parents for even in death people are betrayed, because they obviously had their reasons unless of course they just went crazy, unless they got drunk right after delivery and spoke to God perhaps and talked about how things weren't working out for them and how one day they might move to Alaska and start fresh since there was so much opportunity for a new start there so that's what they would do.

Once she was born they would move to Alaska except they never did, things went back to normal, they sobered up and realized they weren't going anywhere not because they didn't want to but because they were stuck in the mud of their existence and more often than not desire has wheels so instead of leaving they named her Alaska, because every time they called her name it would keep the dream alive, the whole world would come alive in her except it would also be dead at the same time which could definitely drive someone crazy, even perhaps to an untimely death.

"Don't you think so?" she asked. She was obviously being too hard on herself, I thought. Also, there was something different about her eyes when she said all this. And her voice too. This was Alaska talking now and not Al. She was quite outside herself. There was now this exotic and unpredictable turn in her imagination which threatened our whole relationship. Needless to say, it had to stop. I couldn't have her speaking like this to our neighbors, telling them about stuck in the mud existences and desires without wheels. They'd think we were both crazy and drive us out of the neighborhood. I liked this neighborhood and I wanted to stay in it.

"Don't you think you might be getting carried away with all this?" I asked. "Don't you think you might be overreacting? Don't you think there might be a much simpler explanation to all this?"

"I don't know," she said. "There's much more behind this than we think. I wasn't named Alaska for nothing you know."

Her eyes were making me nervous again. They were the eyes of someone possessed, of someone no longer satisfied with focusing just on the surface of things but of someone who had to get inside of them.

For example, whenever she spoke to me now I felt naked. Not in a conjugal way but in a human way I had never been with her before, in a way that exposed too much of me that wasn't flesh, in a way that made me want to cover my chest or the pit of my stomach rather than my genitals.

My genitals were out of the picture entirely. I couldn't see myself using them with her again. She was my judge not my lover. I felt naked, condemned, worthless; I wanted to strike her, I wanted to run for my checkbook and remind her of my balance, of the enormous financial potential of our days ahead. My God, I thought, this was no time to start measuring the worth of each other's soul; there'd be plenty of time for that once the children were grown and out of the house.

"I think this name has something to do with my destiny," she continued.

Destiny! I thought. Didn't I promise her all the destiny she could handle? We were just settling down to a new life together in a new house with new neighbors who made less money than I did which now was 40,000 per with the potential for much much more. Could she be implying that her destiny was somehow different than mine? Wasn't it after all a joint destiny? A destiny laid out in the family plan? I even remembered an article I read which frightened me that said that young couples were starting to take out what they called "destiny insurance" just in case that which was meant to be never is.

"Look," I told her. "It's just a name. There is no destiny in a name."

"What would you know about destiny," she answered back. "Your name is Ray. There is no destiny in the name Ray."

"Maybe you're right," I said. "And maybe you're not. So why worry about it? Let me take you down to city hall tomorrow and we'll change your name. Which one would you like? How about Alice? This way people can still call you Al and not be the wiser."

"Impossible," she said. "It's too late."

"Too late for what?" I asked.

"For us," she said.

I couldn't understand why it was too late for us. If she wanted to keep the name, fine, I could live with it, it never bothered me in the first place. But why was it too late for us?

"You wouldn't understand," she said.

"Yes, I would."

"No, you wouldn't. Just by saying you would automatically means you wouldn't."

"I don't understand," I said.

"I know that," she said. "And even if you did it wouldn't make any difference."

"Why?" I asked.

"Because it's too late."

"Then maybe it is," I said and stormed out of the house.

I went to a bar. I told the bartender my wife's name was Alaska. He asked if she was born there and I said no.

"Well then that's pretty weird," he said and then I left.

On the way home, I stopped at my friend Jerry's house. Jerry's wife's name was Barbara. No problem with that, I thought. Jerry was a very lucky man. Maybe some of this luck would rub off on me.

"Did you know Jerry," I told him once he had gotten used to the idea of having been disturbed and had finally resigned himself to the fact that it was I sitting opposite him now and not his television, "that my wife's real name was Alaska?"

He laughed and then I could hear his wife Barbara laughing all the way from the kitchen. Once Jerry finally stopped laughing he said: "Why?"

"I don't know," I said. "Because she wasn't born there."

"Then don't you think you oughta find out?"

"Why should I find out," I asked him. "What the hell difference does it make?"

"Look," he said. "You came to me. I didn't come to you."

"You're right," I said. "This thing is just driving me nuts."

Then Barbara came out of the kitchen and sat down with us. She came in wringing the towel she had been drying the dishes with. Jerry seemed more disturbed now than when I walked in. I figured he must have wanted to give me some advice about Alaska or about women in general.

"I couldn't help overhearing," Barbara said.

"No kidding," Jerry said.

"Then what do you think," I asked her.

"Maybe it has to do with her destiny,"she said. "Maybe she is destined for more than what she's got. My name is Barbara and all I do is wash dishes all day. Maybe with a name like Alaska you're supposed to do something else, something big!"

"Don't listen to her," Jerry said. "She is crazy."

"No, I mean it," she said. "Maybe I'll change my name too. Maybe I'll change it to Asia. Yes! Asia! Would you like that Jerry? From now on you can call me Asia."

"The hell I will," Jerry said.

"Oh, you will all right," she said.

Then she got that same crazy look in her eyes that Alaska had and she put her face right smack up against Jerry's and just kept repeating her new name over and over again, "Asia! Asia! Asia!" and then Jerry turned his face towards me and said,

"Look, Ray, I don't want to be unfriendly or anything but maybe you better keep all this to yourself," and I said I would and then got up and left and even two blocks down the road I could still hear his wife yelling her new name at him.

When I got home, Alaska seemed a lot calmer and told me she had been thinking about it and had decided to change her name.

"You don't have to do this," I said.

"Yes, I do," she said. "Because you want me to and I want you to be happy."

"What about us?" I asked. "Don't you want us to be happy?"

"Of course. That's what I mean. Us." But there was something wrong. I couldn't quite pinpoint it, but it was there.

"It's really very simple," I told her. "It's just to change a few letters and I'll be with you the whole time."

"Will it hurt?" she asked.

"Not at all," I said. "Just a little paperwork and it's all over."

"Then I'll do it," she said.

The next morning, trying to pull out of the driveway, we found ourselves blocked by an angry mob of sign-carrying women. They were neighborhood women and they looked to be somewhere between sleeping and waking as if they had just been ripped out of their beds by an urgent collective phone call. No doubt they were coffeeless, no doubt they had forgotten their children and left them in their beds.I was frightened but Alaska hardly seemed to notice.

"Stay calm," I told her. "We'll get out of here if I have to run them down."I never once considered running them down. After all, mad or not, they were my neighbors, people like myself and just as entitled to wake up on the wrong side of the bed if they wished and besides one does not run down his neighbors unless he absolutely has to. But why us? Why did they choose our driveway to block?

Then I noticed her as they began to move closer. Actually, it was the one leading the pack who began to move closer, the first one to actually enter our private driveway. It was Jerry's wife Barbara who stood there wringing that same dish towel as the previous evening when she had first changed her name to Asia, wringing it with the same breathless anticipation of a strangler on his first day. When our eyes first met in the rear view mirror, I knew it was me she was after. I put the car into reverse. Perhaps it would be difficult to run down someone named Barbara, I thought, but Asia was a different story.

Asias had been run over before. Then looking again into the mirror I noticed a sign behind Asia which read: "Free Alaska Now!" and then another behind that one which read "Angela No! Africa Yes!" and still another which read "Ethel Then! Europa Now!"

Then Alaska, who hadn't said a word nor moved now suddenly leaned over and turned off the car.

"Relax," she said. "It's me they want."

"You?" I asked.

"Yes," she said. "Can't you see they're here to save me?"

"Save you from what?" I asked.

"Save me from you," she said.

"So that's how it's going to be, hunh Al?" I asked.

"That's right," she said. "And don't call me Al."

Then she left the car but did not slam the door. She wasn't angry. Calmly, more sure than I had ever seen her, she walked towards the waiting mob. What she saw and what she was thinking was beyond me. I admit that even now I tried to see what she saw, to look at things in a different way. I stared at our house and then I tried to look into it and I saw many different rooms and kids in each room and each one wanting their own little destinies and I got a little scared and just looked at the house again and still it was just a house with a still dead garden in the back.

Then a great cheering went up and I watched again in the rear view mirror as Asia greeted Alaska at the threshold of the driveway and how the women mobbed her crying "Destiny! Destiny! Destiny!" and lifted her onto their collective shoulder, carrying her away, down the block, out of the neighborhood, into the future perhaps, leaving the driveway unblocked for me to drive away, to drive as far away as possible. You see my name was Ray and so what destiny could there be for me?

Cherry Orchard

He never listens. I'll tell him something and a minute later he's asking me about what I just told him. He's infuriating. If he wasn't so good looking, if his parents didn't own that great house with the cherry orchard, if, if, if,…he'd only listen to me.

Once, for instance, I told him, I said, "I have a hairdresser's appointment at 10 so I can't pick up the clams." So we're driving; actually, I'm driving, so the least he can do is listen, but no; he's got his head out the window like a dog with its tongue hanging out, drooling all over the highway, so just once I'd like a car to zoom by and rip off his tongue, just long enough so he'd know what it's like not to have a tongue so no one could listen to him even if they wanted to.

So I'm driving and what he's doing is naming things or better yet reading the names off everything he sees like "Joe's Crab House: All You can eat $4.95," or "Bayview Apartments: Condos and Rentals," or "Construction Next 10 Miles," not even saying anything about them, just reading words off signs like he's showing off he can read, but I think to him words mostly don't mean much unless he's talking and if anything anyone else says ever does get into his brain it probably dissolves in a couple of seconds like human flesh in a vat of acid.

Do I sound angry? You bet I'm angry. I mean no more than two minutes after I tell him I have a hairdresser's appointment at 10 so I can't pick up the clams, he suddenly turns to me, I guess there was nothing left to read along the highway, and he says, "So Angela," he calls me Angela, everyone calls me Angie but he's gotta be different, like he's my father, like he owns me. "So, Angela," he says. "Ya gonna pick up the clams at 10 or what?" I was angry.

"Or what? Or what?" I ask him. "I told you, Tony, I got a hairdresser's appointment at 10 so I can't pick up the fucking clams!"

"Hey, Angela," he says. "What ya gettin' all excited about?"

"You just don't listen, do you, Tony?" "You just don't listen to a word I say."

"Hunh?" That's what he says. "Hunh?" Like he doesn't hear me again. But he's lying. He hears me all right, so I swerve the car and head right for that big tree right off the road near Ditmars Blvd. and that really gets his attention because he actually closes his mouth with his tongue inside of it and then digs his fingernails into the dashboard like it might make a difference, like it might stop the car—those big greasy clam-stained fingernails just digging for dear life into that dashboard like he likes to dig into me sometimes, like he owns me too. But this time he's digging just to save his own ass and not get a piece of mine. Men are so stupid. When you get down to it, they're just good for killing bugs and opening jars and stuff like that.

This time I really feel like killing him, killing the both of us, but the feeling doesn't last that long so I swerve the car just in time to miss the tree except we go into a ditch instead, nothing too serious except we blow a tire because kids must have been down there busting bottles all night.

When the car finally stops, I watch how the blood goes back into Tony's fingernails and how he pulls them out of the dashboard real fast and then looks at me, not like he's angry or anything, but like he does when he knows we're alone together where no one could find us, like nothing just happened, like I didn't just almost kill the both of us, but the opposite like this is just the thing to get him horny, like what doesn't get him horny, so he starts to move his fingers up my dress, digging his fingernails into me like I'm the dashboard and his life depends on it.

The next day, we're sitting together in Tony's cherry orchard. It's not really a cherry orchard but more like a backyard with a cherry tree in it but I like to imagine I'm sitting in a whole cherry orchard, so like I say I love that cherry tree and we're just sitting there, and when I sit there I don't feel like talking, so it doesn't matter if Tony's listening to me or not, but this time it's Tony who says something and what he says is, "Hey ya know we're gonna chop that tree down and put in a swimmin' pool. Won't that be great, Angela? I can do laps."

I'm not sure I'm hearing right so I ask him to repeat it which isn't easy because sometimes he has trouble remembering what he just said in the first place, like he doesn't listen to himself either, but he seems to remember this all right and when he comes to the word "laps" again, I faint.

I mean they have to spill a bucket of ice water on me, and when I come to, the first person I see is Tony and he has that same look in his eyes he had when he first thought we were going to crash into the tree.

"What the hell happened to you, Angela?" he says like I did something wrong, like I inconvenienced him in some way.

"Hunh?" I say, like what the hell are you talking about and then I say, "I don't know. I fainted. I don't know. Can't a girl faint anymore without getting the third degree?"

So Tony says "how can ya not know," so I say, "I just don't, okay?" but I know. I know why I fainted.

It all goes back to Mrs. Varatsky's class in high school. We were reading **The Cherry Orchard** about a woman who hates the idea of giving up her cherry orchard and before the play even starts, her kid drowns in a lake and I remember how I couldn't stop thinking about my own kid drowning in a lake or a swimming pool. I mean I couldn't take the pain. And when I said that all the kids looked at me like I was crazy except Azalea, a girl with green hair and earrings that were really tiny little human skulls, but everyone else kind of smirked after I said the thing about pain until Mrs. Varatsky said it was good to feel that way.

She said, "Angie, that is very sensitive of you."

"But I don't want to be sensitive," I told her. "Why I can't I just be like everyone else around me?"

"Because you're sensitive and they're not," she said.

And now that I think of it, it's really something I should never forget and it was true except for Azalea who was also sensitive, probably more sensitive than I was. Once someone was eating a sandwich with rare roast beef in it and Azalea had just caught a glimpse of it, I mean the sight of it had barely reached her brain, and still she fainted right off.

Tony Hates Azalea. She is everything he hates in the world and more. Sometimes I bring her with me to his backyard where the cherry tree is—I don't tell her anything about imagining it's a cherry orchard because she'll think I'm crazy and all Tony talks about is bulldozers and chainsaws how they will all come one day and chop down that tree and flatten out the place so they can put in a swimming pool and the whole time he's saying this he's looking at Azalea, not talking to her but looking at her, like the bulldozers are going to flatten her out too which is pretty funny since she's so skinny and flat already and I start to wonder if maybe he'd like to flatten me out too who is definitely not so flat.

So after this whole thing on bulldozers which he's saying to nobody but himself, I say to him, "You know, Tony," I say; His real name is Anthony, but I always call him Tony, even when I'm pissed at him and now I'm damn pissed at him, but still I call him Tony although I know it would make him mad as hell if I called him Anthony and I am so close I can feel the A and the n coming out but I don't say it, so I say, "You know what, Tony," I say, "if you flatten out the cherry orchard, I'll leave your sorry ass."

"Hunh?" he says. "What cherry orchard?"

"Never mind what cherry orchard. My cherry orchard. That's what cherry orchard. So I'm just warning you, that's all."

One time I tell Azalea I'm feeling kind of nauseous all the time and she tells me it's probably all those clams I'm eating so she takes me to one of those health food places in Greenwich Village where everything is green and pale including the waitresses.

When the food comes I feel one of those big waves of disappointment hit the bottom of my stomach like this can't be the food, it must be the stuff they put on top of the food which you're supposed to scrape off, but when I see Azalea eating it, I know I'm in trouble, so I sort of swallow everything without really tasting it, like I was holding my nose but not really holding it, and the whole time I'm thinking about Tony and his family sitting around the table eating clams with pasta and sauce and good Italian bread you dip into everything and how here there was nothing to dip into because everything was dry as a bone even though there is nothing in this whole place that even has a bone except maybe the waitresses.

On the other hand, Azalea really seems to be enjoying it which really scares me and makes me think of that movie about the body snatchers and when I ask her if she really likes that stuff, she says, "it's not a matter of liking it or disliking it, it's a matter of health," so I know that if I'm not careful I could be sucked into the kind of world where there might be no escape.

When we finally leave the restaurant, I feel much better because it is a lot brighter and less depressing outside and my nausea is gone and I think of how Tony and his family must be sitting around the dinner table now feeling all bloated and I can't help missing that feeling of being so full you feel you're going to explode.

One night Azalea asks me if I want to go see this play called **The Seagull** by the same guy who wrote **The Cherry Orchard.** The first thing I ask her is if anyone drowns in it, especially a kid, and she says no but someone gets shot but that's okay, and after seeing the play I kind of felt like shooting the guy myself he whined so much and I thought how much Tony would have hated this if he came and how he probably would have kept poking me in the ribs all night saying, "Come on, Angela let's get outta here," or "Are you fuckin' nuts takin' me to somethin' like this?" and I have to admit I was kind of glad he wasn't there except I kept thinking he was and everyime I went to reach for his arm there was Azalea instead with those little skull earrings which made me think about death and having to go back to Queens on the subway.

I mean I knew Tony wouldn't come to the play even if I invited him, not unless the actresses would be wearing wet t-shirts and selling budweisers in the lobby for 50 cents. But I knew I had to ask so he wouldn't say I didn't ask him and while I'm asking him, explaining to him what a play is and everything, Azalea is standing there flapping her arms like a seagull, making these screeching noises like they make on the beach when you're trying to eat, and Tony's ignoring her which is good because any minute I think he's going to crush her like a bug, but the whole time he's looking at me, I'm looking at the cherry tree, hoping someday it'll just bloom, just like that and he says, "Whaddya lookin' at?" and I say, "Hunh?" and he says, "You heard me!" and I say, "The cherry orchard. I'm looking at the cherry orchard," I say even though there is none, because I figure I got a right to my own fantasies, and he says, "Well, not for long because it ain't gonna be here much longer, and it ain't no cherry orchard but just some old rotten tree," and I say, "Fuck you, Tony," and he says, "Fuck you too Angela," and when I turn to walk away everything starts spinning and I feel really funny like I'm going to faint.

But I don't faint and the morning after the play, I don't feel mad anymore, so I go back to Tony's house, but when I get there I see a truck that says, "The Pool Man" on the side of it, and then I see some guy with a big measuring stick right in the middle of the cherry orchard where a pool would go and I'm thinking if I only had a gun but then again I'm not really sure who I'd shoot; there are so many choices, and then Tony comes out of his house with this big smile looking all cocky with clam sauce dripping down his chin and the front of his shirt like I'm supposed to get jealous or something like my whole life I've got to be eating clams or my life is worthless, and the first thing he says to me is, "I knew you'd come back." Just like that, the bastard, "I knew you'd come back," and I'm thinking I should just turn and leave again but I'm also thinking how scared he must have been that I wasn't coming back at all and how he must have seen me from his kitchen window and jumped up before even swallowing his last clam.

So I decide to stay for a while and then Azalea shows up which wipes that smile completely off Tony's face. Then she starts flapping her arms across her body like it's cold outside but it's the middle of summer so it's not that, and then when she starts screeching like a seagull I know what she's doing and she says to Tony, "Too bad you missed a good play last night," knowing he wouldn't have seen that play for nothing. But it's not just that. It's like just by telling him he missed "a good play," the truth being he didn't quite really know what a play is, she's like purposely talking way over his head, like she really wants him to know how stupid he is, which makes me feel, just a little mind you, and for a very short time, kind of sorry for him.

"What play?" Tony asks her, all innocent like, like I never told him we were seeing a play, like I never invited him along, so like now I'm steaming mad again, like I've finally had it up to here with him.

"Right? Angela," he asks me. "What play?"

So the first thing I do is hit him in the chest real hard and I hear this terrible hollow sound like there was nothing inside him, no lungs, no heart, no nothing.

Then Azalea starts laughing and Tony gets this look in his eyes like he might kill her, for real, I know that look, and before I know it, he pushes me aside and goes for her, but then I grab him from behind, giving Azalea time to escape, but she doesn't really escape but just stands there all frozen and I can tell she thinks he's really going to kill her, so I hold on to Tony as hard as I can and he spins me around a couple of times and when he finally stops spinning me I feel so nauseous and dizzy I faint straight away and when I come to, Tony is looking down at me and he doesn't ask how I am but he says, "What the hell did ya hit me for?" in a really concerned way, like not for him but for me.

And it actually seems like he's a little worried about me now. I mean, it's the second time I fainted and God how many times can you faint until even someone like Tony starts to worry, so I say, "I'm okay, Tony, I'm okay," as if that was really what he was asking, and he's just standing there now looking down at me like he's never looked at me before; I could swear he seemed to be thinking about something, like more than just one thing, something where one thought would have to kind of jam up behind another; like there might be two thoughts in his head at the same time, like one right there up front and then another one a little bit farther back inside his head; just in front of that big vat of acid you might say. God, it was kind of scary, like something you couldn't quite explain, like the leaves changing colors or suddenly seeing somebody you just dreamt about the night before.

So I get up and when I start walking away, Tony screams, "Wait! I know!You saw **The Cherry Orchard!** You went to see **The Cherry Orchard** last night! The goddamn Cherry Orchard!"

But of course I didn't see **The Cherry Orchard** last night, I saw **The Seagull**, and Azalea, who is far enough away now so she could make a run for it if Tony comes after her again, is screaming, "**The Seagull**, you asshole! Not **The Cherry Orchard, The Seagull**! You damn Guido!"

But Tony isn't even looking at her let alone listening and then Azalea says to me, "Angie, come on, let's get out of here. The guy doesn't listen to a thing you say. He never did and he never will," like this should be the final straw, like I should leave him now for good, but I'm not so sure, I'm not so sure and all this time Azalea is screeching like a seagull, and Tony's mother's screaming the clams are ready, but Tony is ignoring all of them and he's standing there just looking at me saying, "I did too hear you. Don't you believe me, Angie? You went to see **The Cherry Orchard** where the little kid drowns before the play even starts."

And yeah he's talking about the play, he's talking about that, but it's also like he's talking about something else too, so when he says the word "play" it's like he knows what it means and the way he calls me "Angie," and the way he says, "when the little kid drowns," it's almost too much to take like he's telling me in his way, in Tony's way,that he loves me and wants to get married and have kids and not just a cherry tree but a whole orchard with no pool, and I start feeling nauseous again, I mean really nauseous like something is up, like something is really up and I say to him, I say, "Yes, Tony, you're absolutely right. We did see **The Cherry Orchard** last night, we saw **The Cherry Orchard**!" and then I kind of half faint, I mean I'm still kind of awake, at least I think I was, I mean I seem to remember Azalea with her mouth open like she felt she was entering some kind of world where there might be no escape.

And then it's funny because it feels like my nausea is a whole person now and it's standing there in front of me and I know deep down it belongs to me and I begin to cry and Tony, I think it's Tony, for a moment I think it's the pool man or some guy with a chainsaw but no, I'm sure it's Tony, and I hear Azalea who is a tree now, a small tree with her branches spread to the sky and she says, "She's crying because she's sensitive," but that's not it. I know what it is. I know why I'm crying. It all goes back to the time Tony and I were in the ditch together and he wouldn't listen to a word I said.

TELEPATHY

I met Telepathy one day while jogging around the lake. It was a cold and drizzly day and she leaned against the railing of the bridge that stood above the lake and stared at the dead fish floating unremarkably upon the surface. I jogged often, but slowly. It seemed everyone ran faster, more determined, unable or unwilling to keep down with me. I was in no hurry, I was filled with uncertainty and indecision, and my running showed it. I often liked to look at women as I ran and this slowed me down. Nature is good to look at too but you can just take so much of dead fish and the gulls, those beautiful white gulls with their pudgy necks that flew off in panic as I approached.

Getting back to women, though I had never seen her before, Telepathy looked particularly good that day. Nature dulled in comparison. The gulls stood on the railing next to her and stared. She worried them. They couldn't seem to figure her out what she could possibly see in those dead fish. She made them feel very uncomfortable and yet they wouldn't move. She was a threat to Nature because she stood there in the rain trying to learn its secrets. Telepathy had her coat open and it fluttered in the wind like one great wing itching to take off. The gulls too were getting wet but they didn't look as good wet as Telepathy did. This woman is...but before I could even think exactly what she was, she called out to me, "You're right, I am!" and that's how we met.

But that was the last time I really guessed right about her. One night we went to a party given by some friends and we were sitting around having a conversation and there was a supervisor or two from work sitting in this group and they were talking and telling jokes, forcing everyone to laugh, even though I could never quite hear the last line of the joke and always had to pretend I did or else I had to push my head further into the circle where the smell of onion dip on people's breaths had gathered, yet despite this, this dipping of my head into the group smell gave me just the necessary pained look to be able to simulate interest in the conversation. Telepathy sat next to me and when I finally withdrew my head from the middle, she whispered to me:

"That man hates you." "Which man?" I asked her.

"The man sitting opposite you hates your guts and would rather see you choke on a cracker than leave this party alive."

"That's impossible," I told her. "That's Jerry Blaine, my immediate supervisor who taught me everything I know. I've been to his house. I know his kids."

"I know that," she said. "And I also know he hates your guts and that I don't want to be at this party anymore."

I couldn't believe it. Jerry Blaine had been nice to me all evening. At about ten P.M. I remember spilling a drink on him and he just laughed it off.

"There are more suits where that came from," he said.

Perhaps there was a warning in this. Didn't he, only minutes earlier, before some unknown force corralled us into this unearthly circle, compliment me on my input at the company? Yet, Telepathy insisted that he harbored ill feelings towards me all evening.

"Excuse me," I told the group. "My girlfriend has suddenly taken ill and I have to take her home."

"That's too bad," someone said. "Which one is your girlfriend?" I pointed to Telepathy. Jerry eyed her suspiciously.

"That's too bad," someone else said, someone I had never spoken to in my life.

"Couldn't your girlfriend take a taxi? We were enjoying your company so much."

"That's impossible," I said. "My girlfriend isn't feeling very well and I'm afraid she's going to have to be removed from the party."

"To be removed by whom?" someone said as if I had handed him the wrong requisition orders back at the company.

"Couldn't someone else take her home?" a man said, a man from the company I had only seen from the back of the head until tonight. "One time my wife got sick at a party and I had someone else take her home. I ended up having a terrific time!"

"It's different, they're not married," someone else said.

"Her eyes do look a bit glazed," the man with the back of his head turned away from me said.

"It could have been the dip," one of the woman managers said while purposely dipping her celery into it. "Dip can be devastating if not properly digested," she said with just a titter of dipsomania.

This whole time Telepathy said nothing, but her eyes looked like they did that morning at the lake when she tried to look into the souls of the dead fish.

"You see," I said, pointing to her. "I'm afraid I'll have to take her home after all."

Jerry looked at me as if he knew all along I was capable of such outrage, such breach of human decency.

"Who the hell do you think you are?" he suddenly said. "Don't you realize that positions are being determined here as we speak? Is that what you would like me to understand? That you of all people who has not had an original idea in five years shouldn't know better than to jeopardize his entire future over a woman who has been in a catatonic state since eight o'clock this evening onion dip or no onion dip?"

I looked at Telepathy.

"I told you," she said.

The whole next day Jerry was very cold to me. At one point he pulled out the plug of my computer, wiping out five years of work and not once apologizing for it.

"Don't worry," he said. "You won't need it." I realized then and there that the business world was not for me. Telepathy had told me that very thing the moment we returned home last night. She just seemed to know everything before it happened.

"Jerry Blaine wanted my ass," she said.

"Is that why he ruined me?" I asked. "It doesn't matter," she decided.

She thought I should be an artist. So all day I sat before a blank canvas and she would imagine the masterpiece I would paint or I would ponder over a blank notebook and she would imagine the novel I would write. The next day I sat blankly before the same canvas and painted nothing until Telepathy came home and told me that what I had simply done was to paint one of the great masterpieces of all time. Certainly, the canvas was blank, my own mind was blank, but yet she insisted.

"What is it?" I asked her. "Describe it to me." She couldn't she said. At least not in a way that would do it justice. "Was it abstract?" I asked her.

"No," she said.

"Then what is it?" I insisted.

"It's nothing," she said. "You wouldn't understand."

"But it's my painting," I told her. "What right do you have to keep my own painting from me?"

"I'm sorry," she said.

"Sorry?" I answered. "Don't I at least have the right to know what it is I've painted? Or what it is I haven't painted?"

"Look at it!" she screamed. I looked at the blank canvas. "It's your painting! Can't you see what you've done?"

"Maybe," I said. "Maybe if I could just use some paint. Maybe then I could…"

"No!" she stopped me. "That would ruin everything."

The whole next day I stared at the blank canvas that Telepathy said was my masterpiece. It did nothing for me. It was just a big blank piece of nothing. Perhaps I should start over I thought. But this time without the canvas. The canvas was distracting. It tampered with my vision. I would be much better off using blank space. I thought for the first time that I was onto something but Telepathy got angry. She figured I was mocking her, as well as my own talents. I suppose she was right. Try writing the novel, she told me. It will get your mind off the painting. True, I had plenty of paper. I had stolen five years worth from the company. Everyone at the company stole paper. But that's only because they were thieves and not because they wanted to write novels.

But this time I was determined to do it. Unlike the canvas, I would not leave the paper blank. I would put words on it. And when Telepathy came home that night I showed her the first ten pages of my new novel. It was about the life of a clairvoyant living in New York City. She hated it.

"Why do you insist on writing about something you know nothing about?" she asked me.

"I know you," I told her but she knew that wasn't true. "It's garbage," she said. "It's the ranting of a madman. Take my word for it."

"Why should I?" I asked. "You're the one who liked that painting!"

She said nothing. She looked at me. Then she looked inside of me. It was that look again. I felt as if the fly of my soul was open.

"Anything wrong?" I asked her.

"I just read your novel," she said.

"What novel?" I asked.

"The one you haven't written yet," she said.

"Any good?" I asked her.

"A masterpiece," she said.

"Is there anything I can do?" I asked.

"No," she said.

"Why not?" I asked.

"Because you have to understand something," she said.

"What?" I asked.

"That you, like most of my former lovers, are incomplete."

"Incomplete?"

"Yes, and I suppose I'll just have to make the best of it," she said.

"You will?" I asked.

"Yes," she said. "The burden always falls on me."

"And when will I be complete?" I asked.

"That's up to you," she said. "But it won't be in our lifetime."

For the next few days, I missed work terribly. Not the work I was doing, I hated that, but the hours I sat doing nothing but sitting in my little cubicle and harboring deadly thoughts about my co-workers. I missed hiding my thoughts from other people. It's really what made life bearable. Even people trying to guess what I was thinking made me uneasy. And now I spent all my time with a person who could not only read my thoughts but know them years before they were to be formulated. She knew what mood I'd be in all day before I would even wake up in the morning.

"Well aren't you in a foul mood," she'd say to me just as I was opening my eyes that day for the first time.

Sometimes I'd go back to sleep and ask her to wake me up when she thought I was in a better mood. When I finally did get up I found exactly what I wanted for breakfast waiting for me, the exact number of eggs, the exact number slices of bacon, of toast I wanted. Sometimes I'd try to throw her off the track.

"I wanted cereal!" I'd cry. "I wanted Kellogg's Cornflakes!"

"Liar!" she'd cry back. "A relationship cannot survive on lies!"

She was right. Who was I fooling? Besides, I would have been heartbroken if she took back the eggs. She knew everything. She knew when my arteries would first begin to clog or when my cells would begin to multiply at breakneck speeds. She knew the workings of my body as well as my soul. At a Jeans store she said once: "Make sure you buy those pants one size larger because next year you will be three pounds heavier."

Telepathy thought I was OK in bed, at least in the beginning, but after a while she grew bored. Then she grew frightened. Once I reached out for her in the middle of the night and she said, "Don't touch me. Our children would be mutants."

This was her way of letting me know our love life was over. I suppose it was for the best. How could I possibly satisfy a woman who was having sex wired to her from telepathic hunks all over the world? This was only a wild hunch on my part, which she denied, but for which she was extremely proud of me for thinking.

"Thank you for trying to read my mind," she said. "It shows you care."

Of course I cared. Otherwise, I would have thrown her out months ago, which I suppose I never thought about, not even unconsciously, or else she would have had her bags out by now without me having to say a word. The trouble was Telepathy wanted me to think like her. So one day I made a deal with her. I told her that all day I would try to think like her if she would try to think like me. "Is that possible?" I asked her. "Could you do that for me? Just for one day?"

"I'll try," she promised.

So what she did was sit at my desk and write down the names she had made up for all the dead fish she had seen floating upon the surface of every lake she had ever looked into from the railing of a bridge.

"This will quiet my mind," she said. "It will stop me from thinking."

I on the other hand, as I had promised, tried to look deeply into the secret nature of things. Moments later, the doorbell rang. I expected Telepathy to call out to me as she always did and say something like, "Tell him to come back tomorrow at 9 A.M." or "He's going to want $7.49 C.O.D.," or "If she's selling the stuff with the blue gel, buy it!" Or sometimes she'd just say, "Don't answer it! Whatever you do don't answer it!" but this time she said nothing and went to the door to answer it herself. Was it some kind of a surprise? I wondered. After all it was my birthday and perhaps she had ordered a surprise.

On the way to the door she looked at me and asked "Do you know who it is? Do you have any idea who it is?"

I wanted to. I struggled to know, all day I struggled to know what lurked behind closed doors, what secrets lay within the petrified gills of dead fish but alas I could not. "No I don't," I said. "I have no idea."

The bell rang again. It seemed urgent. This much I did know. She looked at me with the same hopeless look as always and she said, without hesitation, "Well then, neither do I!" But I knew she was lying. She too had struggled all day not to know as I did, but to unknow, to see nothing, to know nothing past the first unsuspecting moments of the day. But she too had failed. I saw that. In the normal non-empathic way of humans figuring things out, I truly knew that.

"I'll answer it," I said. "It's the least I can do."

"No, she said."I'll answer it. "It's the least I can do too."

"No, me," I said.

"Happy Birthday!" she cried reaching for the knob and when I heard the blast of the shotgun and watched her drop, I knew she loved me more than any other woman I had ever known. I bent over her watching whatever strange stuff it was that could look into the souls of dead fish fade out of her eyes forever. And when I looked up again there was Jerry Blaine, my old boss, smiling, with his arms stretched out as if to welcome me back into the embrace of an unpredictable universe.

The Hotel Clerk

There was something horrible about Germans laughing. Not knowing any German, he couldn't see what was so funny. He was on a German tour bus going from Frankfurt to Munich. For five hours he would sit and listen to the tour leader, a young, blonde German with the first two buttons of his shirt open, telling exciting stories about Munich, and through it all, he could not understand a word. And how did he know that from time to time they were not laughing at him? He did not notice anyone looking at him, not at any time, but still he knew that Germans were very disciplined and could make things seem very different than the way they actually were. After all, how did he know he was actually going to Munich? Because some German travel agent told him so? Because the tour leader, who could barely speak English, assured him he was on the right bus going to Munich?

He was hot and tired and thirsty and dreamed of biergartens under a hot sun, of intensely blonde German women serving him stein after stein of cold beer. He was more thirsty now than he could ever remember. Even more than the time he had ridden his bicycle around the Grand Canyon and had forgotten to bring water.

Suddenly, he heard yodeling coming from somewhere in the back of the bus. It frightened him. It meant the Germans were not behaving themselves, that chaos had broken out and that unless he joined in, unless he too yodeled at top of his lungs, he would be left in the next service area and forced to hitchhike his way to Munich or at the very least back to Frankfurt.

But his fears were premature. The yodeling was merely one German woman's attempt to wake the tour leader who had fallen asleep in the front of the bus. She too was thirsty. "Wasser! Wasser!" the woman cried out and again everyone laughed, the same hearty laugh that came from deep in the bosom of happy Germans on vacation. He felt better. Perhaps he too would order a drink. After several drink orders had been called out, the tour leader leapt to his feet, wiped the sleep from his eyes, and proceeded to walk up and down the aisles handing out bottles of beer and water to people who it seemed had not even ordered them.

He looked at the Germans drinking. He noticed their long, hard swallows, how they drank with the confidence of a people for whom thirst was never a problem. And now he never felt more alone. When he finally did raise his arm, when he finally did make eye contact with the tour leader, who looked at him with the terrible fear and resentment of a man who might soon have to speak a language he did not know, when he finally muttered the words, "a beer please," he was promptly informed they were out of everything.

"Of everything?" he asked the tour leader.

"Of everything!" the tour leader repeated with the pride of someone who has put down a man in the man's own language. So he decided he would sleep again. He dreamed of the same biergarten, except this time the waitress had her hair in braids and when she brought him his beer, she blew off the head for him.

When he arrived in Munich, his throat was so parched he could barely speak. "Room 509," the tour leader said to him.

"Five-oh-Nine?" he asked, hoping to elicit some conversation, perhaps an acknowledgement that the tour leader might want to join him for a beer later, point out interesting places to visit on one of those big maps he saw him with on the bus, or perhaps let him know if there was another American around or even some German in desperate need of companionship or at least a cold drink. Oh, yes above all a cold drink. "Five-oh-nine?" he asked again.

"Ja," the tour leader said, looking at him now as if he were not only stupid, but deaf too. So he took the elevator, big enough just for himself and his two bags, and creaked upwards towards the fifth floor. The fifth floor hallway was dark and foreboding, but he had no business or concern with the hallway. It was merely a place to station himself while turning his key in the door.

Yet, when he entered his room, he already yearned for the hallway. At least the hallway held out anticipation as well as a means of escape into one or another of the rooms it faced. But the room itself was a dead end, merely a place for suffocation and regret. For God's sake where was the air? He could already see the long night in front of him, the gasping for breath, the sticking of his head under the bathroom faucet. And how could he come back to such a room after leaving it all day, come back with his head full of memories, soaked in sunlight, glowing with beer? No memories could survive in such a room. No, he would have to leave, he would have to make his thoughts known at the front desk while they were still clear in his mind.

But when he got to the front desk, he could not speak. "May I help you?" the woman said, recognizing him as the sole American among the Germans. If she had found things funny, she too might have laughed at him, but she was a woman who took her job seriously.

"I would like…" he said. "I would like some stamps." She looked at him as if she had caught him in the act. But what act? He wondered. Have I done anything wrong yet? This country does have stamps doesn't it?

"How many stamps will you need?" she asked him.

"I will need five," he said, feeling as if he were trapped within a Berlitz tape.

"And will you like some postcards with that?" She asked him.

He hadn't thought about postcards. He would have to send some postcards home eventually.

"Which ones do you suggest?" he asked her, looking at the small rack of cards next to the desk.

"They are all beautiful. They are all of beautiful things," she insisted, "because Munich is beautiful, ja?"

"Yes," he agreed, knowing she knew he hadn't seen any of Munich yet.

But she would not pick out his cards for him. She would just go so far. He knew that. With tour book in hand, he wondered what it might be like to make love to this woman. He had seen movies with women like this. Women whose severe outlines and stiff postures seem to preclude them from making love but who always surprise you in the end. He noticed her looking at his German guide book.

"What will you look at today?" she asked him.

"I don't know yet," he said.

"You must go then to Dachau," she told him.

"The concentration camp?" he asked in disbelief.

"Ja," she said. "The concentration camp. You must go."

During the trip to Dachau he could not get the hotel clerk's face out of his mind. He knew as the train pulled out from underground and rode along the peaceful, lush German countryside that he could still get off at any time. He did not have to go there today. But the hotel clerk insisted. She said it was something he must not miss. Now what was it? He wondered. Guilt, or some sadistic impulse to send another Jew off to the death camp? Was she oppressor or victim? As the train rocked slowly towards Dachau, he looked out onto the countryside and suddenly realized it was the same landscape, give or take a few farmhouses, a few cows, that thousands of others on their way to die had also looked out upon.

At first he had gone the wrong way. "Is this the train to Dachau?" he had asked an old Chinese man because he thought if he asked any Germans he would offend them. But he ended up offending them anyway, at least the ones who were on the train. "Dachau! Dachau!" he found himself screaming at the Chinese man, who could only sit there and shake his head.

The others on the train, not another Chinese man among them, stared coldly at him. He had committed a faux pas, he knew that. It was not his first. He should have brought the hotel clerk. She would have guided him right there. She would have dropped him off at the front gate. But now he was alone. And thirsty. Damn, he thought. Where was this thirst coming from? And then he realized he still had not had a drink since getting on the bus in Frankfurt early that morning. And before that? He couldn't remember. Perhaps Amsterdam. Suddenly he couldn't remember ever having a drink anywhere. And he was certain too that he was on the train going the wrong way. He was frightened. There was a time that people would have given their right arms to be in his shoes, to be moving away from Dachau rather than toward it. But not him. He was, after all, on vacation. He had an itinerary to follow. And weren't recommendations, especially from natives like the hotel clerk worth more than all the Fodors and Froemmers in the world?

He had hoped to be there by noon, spend about two hours walking around the camp, and then get back to Munich for a cold beer and maybe a museum or two. He didn't recognize any of the stops. Germans got on and off the train with a smug familiarity that nagged at him. He looked at his S-Bahn map. Yes, he was going the wrong way. The map indicated he was heading toward a little airplane that must have been the airport. Now he remembered what he did wrong. They had told him to take the S2 train on platform 1 and he had taken the S1 train on platform 2. He had merely to reverse the order of things and he'd be heading in the right direction. And now, thinking back, he was glad he had gotten lost because straightening himself out showed a resolve he wasn't sure he was capable of, a commitment perhaps to finally turning things around in his life.

For such a long time he had always headed in whatever direction fate or chance or his own fears had turned him. One thing, for example, that always frightened him was death, his own and other people's, and now he was determined to visit a place that specialized in it. In a strange way, he felt good about this. Now he could face up to his two biggest fears about death: the fear of group annihilation, where he would just be one more out of millions, and that of dying completely alone, where no one even knew he existed.

Looking out onto the Munich countryside, he wondered what it might be like out there picnicking with the hotel clerk. He imagined her perfect straightness, the absolute rigidity of her bones, the pasty whiteness of her face and arms contrasting wildly with the soft rolling green landscape. This contrast excited him, appealed to something deep in his nature. Why, he wondered again, why then did she send me where there is no love, where there is only the memory of death and the smell of ashes everywhere? Maybe she didn't like him. Maybe she took one look at him and thought, "Towel thief. This Jew is nothing but a towel thief." Maybe she sent all her suspected Jewish towel thieves off to an afternoon at Dachau. He couldn't say.

Once he arrived at Dachau, he still had to take a bus to the camp itself. He always thought the town was the camp. How surprised he was to learn otherwise, to come out of the station and be greeted by tree-lined streets, little picturesque German houses and the smell of fuchsia everywhere.

Yes, beauty was everywhere; it pumped through his veins. Was a sudden infusion of horror, then, really necessary? And the thirst. Yes, it was still there. It had become a part of him now. Should he at least satisfy that much before entering the camp? No, he thought, this thirst might be just the thing to heighten the effect. For once he entered the camp his thirst would no longer be an ordinary thirst but something special, symbolic, the thirst of millions, a thirst that all the beer in the world couldn't quench.

Yes, now he was thinking clearly. Even the nervous giggling of the American students on the bus didn't bother him. And once he arrived at the camp, even the tourists snapping pictures of each other in front of the crematorium, the ovens, the bunks, the shower nozzles, the blood ditches didn't bother him. He was hot and thirsty; the reflection of the sun off the hot white gravel, the sound of shoes dragging across the sharp rough pebbles, it was as if suddenly he had become a prisoner, a ghost moving slowly among the clean, sterile structures of horror. He felt too he had to urinate, but where in this vast city of torture was he to find a men's room?

He saw people filing into a building which contained a museum filled with photos of people either being murdered or waiting to be murdered. They sold postcards here too. But nothing to drink. When he entered the building there was a flurry of activity. Large photos hung in historical order, but very few people here were able to proceed in any orderly manner. It was as if there was some sort of natural resistance to order. One might find himself looking at the liberation of the camp in 1945 and suddenly get shoved over to a photo of prisoners getting off the trains in 1939. But it didn't matter. The beginning was the end, the end was the beginning. Everything was one crazy historical loop, he knew that. There was a film every half hour, so that you could see the same people getting slaughtered over and over again, the same expressions of surprise, disappointment, terror and resignation all day if you wanted. There was, after all, no supervision, no one to tell you you've seen enough or you haven't seen enough. There were no tours or tour guides, but only signs and arrows, and at one point he followed an arrow to behind the crematorium, to a tool shed whose tools were meant for people to dig their own graves.

And there, much to his astonishment, he saw two people making love. And next to them, right beside their feverish lovemaking, was a bottle of mineral water. He wondered if he might ask them for a drink. Love and Water. Yes, they seemed to have everything.

He thought about women. The more he stared at the two people making love, the more lonely he felt, the more he realized how little love there was in his own life. Yes, he had no one, but did he have to be reminded of it here? Here he had hoped to deal more with the question of universal suffering than his own inability to get laid. And besides, would he ever really want to find love behind the tool shed of a crematorium? When he looked at their naked flesh he realized how naked flesh can burn, disintegrate more quickly than it might take two people to achieve orgasm.

Perhaps they were trying to make a point. Perhaps they were young artists using their own bodies to demonstrate the surviving, eternal qualities of the flesh, perhaps forming themselves into a living sculpture, a symbol of naked love bursting forth out of a field of death. After all, there were plenty of memorials to the spirit, plenty of chapels and synagogues at the camp now, but nothing about the eternal qualities of the flesh. And the water bottle next to them? Part of the exhibit no doubt, for wasn't water harder to find here than even love? He might ask them about this when they were done, for how often did you actually get to ask questions about a work of art with the expectation that it might answer you back?

Yes, most likely he had come upon a new exhibit at the camp, for after all, what did he really know about exhibits or camps? It was a new era, a new world, he thought, but when he looked over again at the couple, they had stopped moving. Was it over? Would they start again in half an hour like the film at the museum? He wondered still whether he should ask for some water, but before he could speak, one of the figures, the one on top, raised itself slowly, grabbed the bottle, and walked into the tool shed. It was the male figure, and now he could see the other, the woman, much more clearly.

She looked quite pleased as she stared up into the brilliant blue sky.

He didn't know what to do. Should he leave without saying a word, or should he introduce himself to the woman, explain why he had been standing there such a long time? "I am not a voyeur," he would tell her. "I am an art lover."

But he couldn't speak. Instead, he cleared his throat, a foolish thing to do really, a sign of contempt if there ever was one. The woman looked at him. Now, for the first time he began to feel excited, excited in a way that no piece of art could make him, and he had to remind himself where exactly he was.

"You ought to try it sometime," the woman said to him. "It's quite liberating."

He felt embarrassed as if the exhibit had turned on him, mocked his intellectual pretensions, if not his obvious lack of sex.

"I was just wondering if I might have some of your water," he said to her.

The woman laughed in a heavy, guttural way and suddenly he felt as if he were the one who was naked. "He just took it away," she said. "Didn't you see that?"

"Yes," he said. "I understand." But he didn't understand. Not any of it. If this was indeed an exhibit than why was it talking to him? Where was everyone else? Was it only for him? Had the hotel clerk set this all up to humiliate him? Perhaps the answer was in the tool shed with the man and his water. He walked toward the shed. The woman made no move to stop him.

"May I?" he asked her just before stepping over the threshold of the shed.

"Be my guest," she said.

When he entered the shed he was able to make out the face of the man sitting naked amongst a collection of farm implements, with a shovel in one hand and the bottle of water in the other. He recognized him immediately as the tour leader who was always quite dressed except for the two open buttons of his shirt.

"So you found me," the tour leader said to him.

"I wasn't looking for you," he told him.

"But you found me anyway."

"By accident," he said.

"But isn't everything in life just an accident?" the tour leader asked him.

He thought about this. Perhaps this was true, yet did he want to go back into a bus with a tour leader who believed in the inevitability of accidents? He didn't know. Was the woman an accident? He noticed how well the tour leader was speaking English now, so perhaps there was a chance to find out why he had been made the butt of so many jokes on the bus. He felt, suddenly, as if certain mysteries, about himself, about his relationship to the tour leader were about to be revealed.

"I wonder," he said. "I wonder…"

"You wonder?" asked the tour leader.

"Yes," he said. "I wonder if I might have some of your water."

"All gone," the tour leader said, turning the bottle upside down.

"Then I suppose I'll be going now," he said to the tour leader.

"Yes," the tour leader said. "Go."

He was disappointed. He hoped the tour leader might call him back. After all, weren't things beginning to point in that direction? Certainly, he himself would never approach the tour leader, not with him stark naked holding the shovel up like that. No, he was quite unapproachable, just like everyone else he had met.

"And do not forget!" cried out the tour leader.

His heart leapt; he braced himself for some penetrating philosophical revelation in perfect English.

"We leave tomorrow no later than 9 in the A.M., Ja?"

He turned around. He looked at the tour leader, naked and holding his shovel in one hand and thought how ridiculous he was and how foolish he was to expect any answers. There were no mysteries, no answers. Only chaos. "Ja, Ja," he said to the tour leader. "Ja Ja."

The whole way back to Munich he grew more and more thirsty. He had spotted a snack stand across the street from the camp but by the time he decided to cross, the bus had arrived and he did not want to wait for another. He had waited this long for a drink, he could wait a little longer. Besides, he did not want to have to stay at the camp any longer than was necessary. It had been a terrible experience. To have seen the grisly sights of a death camp would have been one thing, but to have witnessed his own tour leader screwing some woman behind the crematorium was worse than he ever could have imagined and tomorrow morning he would have to ride all the way back to Frankfurt with a man whose face, among other certain body parts, he would forever associate with the Holocaust.

When he got back to the hotel, the woman who sent him to Dachau was still behind the desk. He looked at her differently now. He tried to imagine her lying naked behind a tool shed under a blazing hot sun. Was it possible? But if he had learned anything that afternoon, wasn't it that anything and everything was possible?

Unless, of course, he imagined it all, imagined the camp, the crematorium, the tool shed, the naked bodies, the snack stand. Even that was possible. People who suffer long bouts of dehydration were known to hallucinate. The only thing he was really sure about was the hotel clerk herself because she was the point from which he left and the point to which he returned. Everything in between was out there someplace or else didn't exist at all. He noticed her now looking at him and jotting something down on a note pad. What could she be writing? "The Jew is back. Watch the towels."? Then she looked up at him and said, "Room 509, ja?"

"Ja," he answered her with confidence. "Room 509."

When he got to his room, he took off his shoes and went right to bed. What a day, he thought, a day of horror and lust, the two things only a native could recommend. He had seen enough of both all right, and even when he closed his eyes he continued to see: the camp, the crematorium, the naked bodies, the snack stand. And suddenly he wanted everything. He wanted to die, to be tortured, to suffer. He wanted to live, to love, to eat, to drink, yes, especially to drink.

He had to calm down. His head was spinning. Damn, he thought now. When he saw those two people screwing he should have called a guard. That was the civilized thing to do, but it was too late now. And was the tour leader planning to do with that shovel, he wondered. Plant a tree?

Then, just before he drifted into sleep, he imagined he saw a white rectangular box-like object filled with gravel somewhere on a deserted road. A refrigerator! He screamed. Was it a dream? Then he jumped out of bed and there it was! "I'm up, right?" he asked himself. "Yes," he said. I am moving around in this room. I am no longer in bed." He looked at the bed and it was empty. The pillow was crumpled. "If the pillow is crumpled then I must have been in bed and now I am out of bed. I am not dreaming," he said. "This is a refrigerator." He had not noticed it before. Perhaps they, perhaps the hotel clerk herself, had brought it in during the day while he was away at the camp.

When he opened the refrigerator, he could not believe his eyes. There was soda. There was beer. There was mineral water. He took out a bottle of soda and rubbed it against his neck. It was cold all right, just as he had always imagined.

He looked for an opener. He was frustrated it wasn't a twist-off, but after all, there must be an opener somewhere. Why would there be soda and no opener? But where was it? He looked everywhere, inside the refrigerator, in the bathroom, on the wall near his bed, everywhere he could imagine a bottle opener might be. Perhaps, he thought, the handle on the refrigerator door might double as an opener. Leave it to those efficient Germans, he thought. But when he tried to pry off the cap with the handle, he only succeeded in putting a large dent in the refrigerator door.

In fact, he soon began to leave dents everywhere, but despite denting nearly every wall and door in the room, still he could not pry the cap off; he could not get a single drop out of the bottle.

He was getting thirstier and thirstier, and thinking now he might actually die of thirst, he decided to smash the bottle open. Yes, things had reached the point now where he would have to smash it open. And then, as if he might be imagining things again, there was a knock on the door. Oh, no, he thought. He was finished now. They must have heard him denting half the room and sent up security agents to take him away. Another knock. He could see the handcuffs flashing before his eyes. A third knock, and finally, after hiding the unopened bottle of soda under the bed, he answered the door. It was the hotel clerk and in her hand, dangling before him, was a small metal object he at once recognized as some instrument of torture.

"Opener?" the woman asked. At this point, he backed further into the room. The woman followed him, closing the door behind him. "I am very sorry," she said. "But it seems we have neglected to provide you with a bottle opener."

"Thank you," he said, taking the opener from her hand. He looked it over. It was a strange looking opener. Certainly, it could have been some instrument of torture, he thought. Perhaps it was meant to do more than just open bottles and cans.

"Would you like me to show you how to use it?" the woman asked him. He wasn't sure what he wanted. The hotel clerk looked different now. She had changed her dress. She was wearing something much softer now, something where he could easily put his hand up the back of or even down the front.

"You have been to Dachau today, yes?" she asked him.

"Yes," he said.

She moved closer to him.

"And what did you think?" she asked, pushing her face against his as if she meant to kiss him.

He thought about the tour leader and the woman making love behind the tool shed. Funny, he thought, how that seemed to have made the biggest impression on him.

"It was terrible," he said.

"Yes," she said, kissing him softly on his lips and then pulling away again.

"Terrible, just terrible."

Perhaps she hasn't noticed the dents after all, he thought, as he put his hand up the back of her dress. Her buttocks felt partly soft, partly hard, partly wet, partly dry, like someone who had been partly sitting, partly standing all day. I am feeling up the buttocks of the hotel clerk, he thought, the same one who sent me off to Dachau this morning.

"Why did you send me there today?" he whispered to the woman, slipping his free hand between her legs.

"I didn't send you," she told him, sandwiching her legs hard against his hand. "I suggested you go."

"Why?" he asked again, forcing his hand out from between her legs and putting it down the front of her dress. All the time he was imagining her dressed as she had been early that morning, picturing her in that brown skirt like the hard shell of an insect it would have been impossible for his hands to penetrate.

"Because I knew you were thirsty," she said.

"Yes," he said. "Very thirsty."

"For love," she said. "I thought you were thirsty for love."

Long after the hotel clerk had left, he remembered the unopened bottle of soda hidden under the bed. He could open it now, he thought. He could open anything now. He looked over at the opener which sat on the night table next to the bed. He remembered reaching for it, fingering it, exploring its strange contours as he made love to the hotel clerk. It was cold and jagged and helped maintain his passion for the woman.

He thought about the tour leader and how he'd like to tell him, tell all the passengers what happened here tonight. He could imagine them all shouting at once, "Ja! Ja! Ja! Ja! Ja!" as the bus rolled back towards Frankfurt. He held the bottle in his hands. It was warm now, but that didn't matter because he was certain there was a refrigerator full of cold beer and soda. But he would wait. He had been thirsty for so long now it had become a part of him, a part of his journey, a part of Munich and Dachau and the naked tour leader and the hotel clerk whose back finally folded in his arms like when you find the right button under an ironing board after searching for a very long time.

Yes, he thought as he looked at all the dents he had made in the walls of a room where memory could not survive, he would take the thirst back with him to Frankfurt and perhaps even beyond that.

The Lamp

One day a friend came to my house and when he saw my desk lamp, one of those really flexible lamps where the light zeros in on just what you're looking at, he said, "You know I've been working on a really difficult passage in my new novel, a passage to end all passages, so I can really use this lamp because mine is broken."

So I lent him the lamp, and at first it wasn't so bad because the first week it was gone I did no work at all, kept away from my desk, and instead, as if I hadn't a care in the world, basked under the harsh fluorescent glare of the kitchen lights. But by the second week I grew restless, and unable to resist work any longer, I dragged out an old lamp from the hall closet, a short, squat lamp my mother had given me, a lamp completely devoid of personality, and placed it in the very spot where my desk lamp had been. But instead of this lamp zeroing in on my manuscript, it resisted it all together, and nothing I did, no matter what position I moved it in, could convince it to do otherwise. Once, out of frustration, I ripped its shade off, but all it did in return was to flood my manuscript with a weak, flaccid light as if to say, "Who feels foolish now?"

And all those days, sitting at my desk, squinting over my manuscript, I thought to myself, "God, I want my lamp back. God I want my desk lamp back." I even imagined that sometime in the middle of the night, the door bell would ring and there would be my friend, desk lamp in hand, saying, "Hey, I just couldn't take this. I mean, you need it, don't you?"

But that never happened and then one night, still squinting, still thinking, "Hey, isn't it about time I got that lamp back?" I started to write my own passage which began something like this:

"I lent my desk lamp to a friend a month ago today, one of those really flexible lamps where the light zeroes in on just what you're looking at and I'm starting to get the feeling that he will never give it back to me. I can tell this by his eyes. They are the kind of eyes that neither receive nor emit light. They are like two dead pools in which nothing can live and where time has no beginning and no end."

Shortly after I wrote this, as if by some miracle, my friend called. "Hi," he said. "I was just thinking about you." To me that sounded promising and I hoped that the next words out of his mouth might be, "I still have your lamp, don't I?" But that didn't happen and instead he said, "I just finished the first chapter of my novel and I'd like you to read it." First chapter! I thought. At this rate he might need that lamp forever. "Okay," I said. "Let me come over and pick it up."

I figured at least I'd be in the same house with my lamp, you know I could kind of hover around it, let him see us together again, make the connection, owner and lamp, so finally something in his head would light up and he'd say, "You know, it just hit me. That's your lamp, isn't it? Well, first chapter or no first chapter you're going to take that back with you today and I don't want to hear another word about it."

But that didn't happen. He never made the connection. When I walked into his house, I could hear the soft, buzzing sound of my lamp from a distant room. He hadn't even turned it off. I wanted to go to it like a mother whose child burns with fever in some stranger's room, but instead I allowed him to steer me straight into his living room while he alone went back into his study to get me the first chapter of his novel.

Sitting in the living room, I noticed the photo on the coffee table that I had seen many times before, the one of my friend posing with a halogen lamp. The fact that they were both thin, that they were both around the same height, and that they both seemed to give off light from the top of their heads, made them look very much like brothers. Looking around now, I couldn't see the lamp anywhere. When my friend came back, in one hand the manuscript, in the other no lamp, I asked, "Who's the Halogen?"

"An earlier time," he said. "Diffused. Unfocused." "What happened to it?" I asked, hoping this might force him to keep thinking of lamps and as a possible consequence of that, my own lamp. "Threw it out," he said. "Once the bulb burnt out, I was in no mood to replace it." He said this with just enough bitterness to make me believe his love-hate relationship with lamps could spell doom for my own.

A few minutes later, after handing over his first chapter, he offered me a beer. I figured, why not? Maybe if I loosened up a little, lost my inhibitions, I'd get the nerve to ask for my lamp back. He brought over two glasses of beer, one glass said, "Ramada Inn—Tucson, Arizona," the other one, the one he gave me, said, "Dr. Tyrone Jaffee, D.D.S." and it had a phone number on the inside of it which became clearer and clearer the more you drank. After this we had another and then another, and though after a while I did manage to memorize the dentist's phone number and even called him twice, still I could not quite loosen up; in fact I even got more uptight, and it seemed the more uptight I got, the looser my friend got until he asked if he could borrow my computer. "No! No!" you can't have it I wanted to say, but after all, he did deserve it since, let's face it, at this point he was the more experienced writer, and without my lamp I wasn't using it much anyway. Still, I wanted to know what it would be like to say no to him and what he would have said to that.

What if he had said nothing, I thought. Then what? Was I to just sit there, staring at those eyes which neither took in nor gave out light and which would only negate my own existence? So I told him, "Sure, why not?" and when I got home, instead of waiting for him to call and remind me about the computer, I called him and told him to pick it up any time he wanted, hoping he would be so thankful, he might tell me he would be bringing the lamp by as well. But then something caught my eye. It was the first line of the first page of my friend's manuscript and it read,

"Today I borrowed a desk lamp from a friend and I have decided
to never give it back. Ask for it back? Don't make me laugh. Tomorrow
I'll borrow his personal computer. On Friday his DVD player, Saturday his
rare book collection, on Sunday his Blackberry and so on and so forth until
I have borrowed everything in his house including his tooth brush."

So this was it, I thought. The passage to end all passages! He is trying to tell me something; he is sending me a message, yes, I would call him right back and he'd say, "So do you see what I'm trying to say? Do you see how foolish it is not to ask for something back which belongs to you and to no one else?" But that didn't happen. Instead he said, "So what do you think? Does it have potential?

Can you see it all happening?" "Yes," I told him. "I can see it now. I really can," and dropping the phone I ran into my bathroom, grabbed the last toothbrush I had to my name and clutched it tightly against my chest.

JOURNEY OF THE FISH

Many times I would find myself completely alone staring into the tank, staring in particular at this one fish, this brown fish with orange stripes that swam around the same miniature mythical city, hour and hour, day after day. I loved this fish; I loved watching him. I loved his relentless pursuit of nothing. Of course I didn't know how he felt pursuing it. After all, nothing means different things to different people, let alone different fish. I did know he never seemed bored. He always seemed to have a purpose. I felt I needed to touch him, to feel him, perhaps to crush him. Any of those things would satisfy my need to be both part of and to disrupt his journey at the same time.

I was a strange child. There were times I was sure the fish was watching me too. Maybe I made his heart pump twice as or God knows how much faster. Maybe I made him move faster, made him expand his lungs to the bursting point, but perhaps more than that I changed his world view. Suddenly, and I was convinced of this, he realized, like in an epiphany for fish, that he was a prisoner, a multi-colored spectator looking out into a distorted and cruel world. As for me, the prospect of touching him, of stopping his endless yet circumscribed journey, if just for an instant, was so exhilarating I could barely contain it in my child's brain. I needed only to confirm its existence and I'd go away. Its vision haunted me. It was the least real thing I had ever seen, even less so than my parents or my brother. Less real even than my own existence.

I knew no one else had ever touched this fish. People didn't touch fish—unless they had to. People had experience with fish, especially dead ones all the time.

They were catching them, sometimes eating them, sometimes throwing them back, but I don't mean that kind of touching.

I remember keeping a journal of my own at that time, a journal relating my own journey towards the great fish. I say great fish because to me it was great, a fish of mythological proportions and that was way before I ever read Moby Dick.

Day 1—We're going to visit my aunt in Middle Village! You know what that means. The fish tank! Am I ready? But when? When do I make my move?

Day 2—I've been thinking and re-thinking this whole thing. I'm only eight so I can't think yet of things in terms of journeys. Especially metaphorically. No, according to my parents this is a trip, a small trip, a visit really, and whatever they say goes. But the point remains, what exactly is my intention? I have this over-whelming urge to touch this fish, I know that, but what do I hope to get out of it? Sometimes it feels sexual. Like up in the country when my parents caught me and this girl pulling our pants down together behind the laundry. It felt good up until the time they caught us and then it felt terrible and my parents said it was terri-ble, so that was bad and this has that kind of feeling to it like if I get caught it would be similar to getting caught with the pants down. I'd be labeled a weirdo for life, a strange child who touches fish and god knows what else who'd have to wash his hands constantly and worst of all the word, just the word "fish" would never be allowed to be spoken in our house again. But the point is that the feeling right before pulling my pants down and the feeling I get when I think about put-ting my hand in the fish tank are almost the same.

Day3—It's official. Tomorrow we're going to Middle Village. ETA 3 P.M. I can't get the fish or the fish tank out of my head all day. The anticipation is kill-ing me. I try to watch cartoons, read comic books, even stick my head in the toi-let but nothing works.

Day 4—All night I dreamed I was swimming in a fish tank and a giant face kept looking through it, at me and I was thinking, oh yeah, just try it—Other fish kept swerving out of my way slamming their bodies against the side of the tank. What idiots, I think to myself. Then, suddenly, a giant hand drops itself into the tank and I notice it's my hand because it's got that scar on it from when that kid stuck me with a pencil in the first grade and I start screaming but I'm a fish so I can't scream, only squirm and I see my mythological city, my only refuge dissolving in the background and then I wake up having to pee very badly, in an astronomical sort of way, and my mother is standing over me and says, "Bad dream?" and I say, "Yes, bad dream." But I won't mention the word fish.

Day 5—2:00 P.M. We all pile into the car. Me and my brother, my mother, and of course, my father, the pilot, the navigator, the admiral, the general—he's got his big cigar all ready to light it up at the first red light like always. We stop for gas. Actually, he stops for gas. The rest of us have nothing to do with it. WE trust him to know how much gas he needs. Sometimes we notice the needle is on the "E" and he says, "That means 'enough'" so we know to keep quiet. We start to smell the gasoline and my mother says, "God, I love that smell," and we all agree it's a wonderful smell, one of those things that smell better than they taste, like coffee or burnt toast. The gas attendant cleans the windows and when he finishes everything has this smeared distorted glow to it like our eyes have gone slightly bad but at the same time the world has brightened.

The attendant asks my father if he should check the oil and my father says okay because he thinks the guy's doing him a tremendous favor, a favor larger or at least equivalent to life itself, like my father's a big shot and he's privileged to get asked about his oil. So the guy puts a big stick in the engine and when it comes out it looks exactly like it did when it went in but the guy says, "You're a little low."

My father looks at him funny and then straightens up. I think of the water in my aunt's fish tank and her never checking it so that the fish start to dry up. "Fill it!" I yell over to my father as if filling his tank will make people fill things up everywhere that need to be filled up. It's like my father is suddenly in control of all that.

"Okay, fill it up," he says to the attendant. I am happy because I can only be happy if things are filled to their capacity like the reservoirs. Then my father asks him to check the tires and I'm getting worried he might ask him to check everything but one of the tires does need air and the sound of air going into the tires is so fulfilling, like life beginning all over again everywhere.

My mother, after being quiet for a long time, finally says, just when my father pays for everything and is ready to pull out, "Where's the cake? Is the cake in the back seat?"

We don't see a cake anywhere. It turns out it's still on the kitchen table at home. That would have been my last guess. That seemed inconceivable to me. But we head back home, nevertheless.

2:45 P.M.-We pile back into the car. Me and my brother switch places. I have a new view. We stop at the red light and my father re-lights his cigar. He puffs extra hard this time. His face turns as red as the light. I'm worried. I figure another 100 times of this lighting and re-lighting his cigar and he will die. At the same time I have this terrible fear that my fish may no longer exist, that maybe my aunt has gotten rid of the tank. Gas tanks, fish tanks, father, fish, my fears become entangled. I feel cranky and start whining.

"When are we going to get there already?" I ask. My brother tells me to shut up. It's good to hear his voice. He hasn't spoken a word in two days.

2:47 P.M.-My father leans over and says something to my mother.

"You're kidding," she says.

"Why would I kid about something like that," he says.

"Can't it wait?" she asks. "We're practically there."

"No we're not," he says. "We're not even on the highway. And there's traffic."

"Then let's forget the whole thing," my mother says. "I'll call when we get home and tell them we're not coming."

Then my father turns around in the middle of traffic. Horns blast from every direction. He curses all of them. I don't quite understand what's going on. It's like the end of the world. I feel like I'm in a fish tank and the world is swirling around us.

"Stop!" I cry out. "Stop!"

"Crybaby!" my brother yells out.

Then, suddenly, we're home again. My father runs out of the car. My brother starts crying.

"Oh, God," my mother says. "That man is impossible."

What man? I wonder. And how can a man be impossible? Is the fish impossible too? Does impossible mean ungraspable? I remember my teacher saying ungraspable meant something impossible to grasp. Everyone laughed because it sounded funny. But not me. I didn't laugh because it scared me. I thought of the fish. My fish. I concentrate very hard on the fish but I can't picture it now. I can't picture my aunt either. Suddenly, I can't remember what my aunt looks like. I tell my mother I want to go see my aunt because I can't remember what she looks like. I mean the fish too, especially the fish, but I won't mention fish.

"Don't worry," she says. "We'll go. If you're father ever gets back, we'll go."

It seems like we've been waiting for days. Neighbors pass by and stare into the car, looking at us funny like we were in a tank and we stopped swimming, that just like that we went dead.

"Where's daddy?" I ask.

"He must be reading," she says. "I know him. He sits there and reads. Meanwhile…" she says.

"Meanwhile," I think to myself. I always loved the word meanwhile. It's a word they use all the time in comic books in the big supplements that cost 25 cents. It is a word of great complexity implying that things are happening all over the place at the same time, great journeys and adventures overlapping each other.

This is what our journey to my aunt's house is like. My mother practically implies it right here. It is taking on a journey of great human not to mention ichthylogical proportions. A tropical fish, abandoned in some lagoon in the Bahamas or some place like that and then whisked to some crowded pet store tank in Queens where my aunt buys it and then drops it, untouched, into her own fish tank in Middle Village. This tropical fish, no more than an inch long, yet as large as a child's imagination, always moving in circles, searching endlessly, hopelessly, for its point of origin.

Then, just as my mother says "meanwhile…" for the third or fourth time, my father re-appears looking somewhat repentant, but relieved which I hope will make him a more conscientious and more focused navigator.

He backs up and tears out of the parking lot. Until that moment I had only heard about people who tear out of places but now I witness it myself. He nearly passes three red lights—I think they were solid yellows—and then my mother tells him to slow down we don't need a ticket to add…but it's too late.

We're stopped. The cop is nice. He says something about his uncle having corns after my father tells him he's a podiatrist but he gives him the ticket anyway.

"That light was clearly red," he tells my father, almost apologetically as if only it could have remained yellow just a little longer, but the law is the law and my father knows it. He does not argue.

My mother, on the other hand tells the cop she thought it was a still a bit yellow, kind of the outside edges of it, a kind of afterglow you might say, pink really, but the cop ignores her and leaves. My mother turns to my father and says,

"That light was a red as your face. If we get there in one piece it will be a miracle." Fish know time. The fish must be wondering where I am I thought. Fish know time. They don't need watches or clocks, they depend on shadows and light.

4:15: We finally arrive. I get this nervous feeling, like butterflies in the bottom of my stomach. My aunt had been worried about us. All the other guests gather around us as if we were shipwrecked souls back from the dead.

"Traffic," my mother says.

No one has eaten yet. The turkey, the potatoes, the corn, are all still in the oven. My uncle has plied the men with schnaaps. The women talk excitedly about whatever women speak excitedly about, something mysterious but I can't understand it.

4:17: I search for the fish tank. I'm sweating and my mother knows it. I see her eying me from another room. Then others eye me as well. Suddenly, people start asking me how I am, what I've been doing (it's summer so I'm out of school). My aunt begins her usual interrogation about all sorts of things, even whether or not I have a girlfriend.

4:28-I tell her everything just so she'll leave me alone including this rash I saw on my brother's neck this morning (which he doesn't even know about yet because he's just in the beginning scratching stages.) What more can I do?

7:15-The fish have remained untouched by me now for 3 hours. That is 3 human hours. I don't exactly know how long that is for fish but I imagine it must be years. The fish must think I'm not coming. He's probably become complacent. He's slowed his pace around the tank; his heart beats slower, his mind falls back to a light to moderate alert system. If I can just get there in a few more minutes, he's mine!

7:30-Everyone has left except us. No one mentions the fish tank. Does anyone even notice it? I do. I notice it now from a long distance. It looks like it's on fire now, the mythological city is in flames, but I believe it is the reflection of the beautiful Middle Village sunset. Then I see him. The one I want. I wonder now if he knows. All my life people have been telling me that fish know things. They don't know how exactly, but they just know things. That's what people say but I say what do they know about fish? I knew this fish and vice versa. In some strange way I believe he wants to be touched. At least I tell myself that.

7:35: My Aunt and Uncle and my parents are all talked out. It's almost dark out. My brother is dying to go home. I can tell by the distorted way he looks at things, his face all scrunched up like anything not his room is an obstacle to his freedom.

Where the fish tank is now there are no lights and so the tank has disappeared from my view. It is as if it has never existed at all or perhaps it has only existed in my own mind, that it is in my brain. The fish swims round and round and when he stops, for anything, just to catch his breath, I will die.

This sudden realization that perhaps I am imagining things makes me start to sweat because who knows maybe I'm imagining my family as well, imagining everything. I start to feel dizzy too and this my mother notices immediately.

"Are you feeling alright?" she asks me.

"No," I tell her. "I think I'm coming down with a fever."

"Really?" she asks as if I'm kidding.

I remain silent. My mother puts her hand on my forehead and I am convinced by doing so she will kill my fish.

"He does feel a little warm," she says.

"Oh, he's fine," my father says.

"He's a phony," my brother says. "He just doesn't want to go to school tomorrow."

"And you have a terrible rash," I tell him, pointing to the back of his neck.

"Oh my God!" my mother exclaims. "You do!"

"Don't scratch it," my father says.

He applies, of course the same medical reasoning on my brother's neck as he would on someone's foot.

"You want some ointment?" my uncle asks. "I've got some good ointment for that."

"Oh, Ed's got ointment for everything," my aunt says. "Some people collect stamps, he collects ointment."

I never knew this about my uncle. I knew he wore hats indoors and tried to perform a hernia operation on himself once but I knew nothing about the ointment. Ointment, the word, the feel, the very idea of it always frightened me but suddenly I remember the picture of the fish on the tube of Desitin ointment I used to have as a child. I used to think the fish felt like the Desitin. But of course ointment comes from fish. Everyone goes back into the living room while my Uncle goes looking for the ointment. Lights go on everywhere. I see the fish tank.

7:45: At first I go into my Aunt and Uncle's bedroom with them. No one has been in there for years. I even doubt my aunt and uncle have ever been in here or at least not for a long time. Everything smells like ointment or what I think ointment might smell like. Then, as my uncle rummages through his ointment drawers looking for just the right kind for my brother's rash, a back of the neck ointment as opposed to a front of the neck one, I begin to sneak out of the room.

It is a cavernous room with a very faint sunlight, as if light has been bent, refracted, reflected several times over before reaching here, terribly weakened and abused by dark heavy objects. I can barely make out my aunt's face in this light. She could be a thousand other people. She could be Chinese. And then there's the tank just outside the bedroom. Once outside I hear voices.

"Don't scratch it, it will become infected." And then the recriminations, the innuendos.

"Where did you get that? Where have you been? For Godsakes what did you touch!"

This last one frightens me. I think of this fish and my own neck. Could my brother have gotten to this fish, any fish before me? Impossible, I think. Even he couldn't think of such a thing. This is my journey, invented only by and for me. No one else knows about it or could ever imagine I would imagine such a thing. And besides, I know for a fact a fish can only cause a rash if you think it will.

8:15: I think it's about 8:15 or so but I can't swear to it. I am in front of the fish tank now. The fish has stopped swimming. It stares at me. It's as if he has been sitting quietly for several hours just waiting for me. Perhaps he's willing to give himself up to me or perhaps he wants to touch me as well. This would change everything for after all whose journey is it? Mine or the fish's?

Finally, as if it had a mind of its own, my hand sinks into the tank. It is cold and other worldly. Fish at first seem stunned, terrified and then swim away in different directions as if I have disturbed the normal pattern of fish, sent them crashing into small rocks, sucking on the end of the air filter. There seems to be among the fish in the tank a general feeling that life has changed, that things will never be the same.

I no longer see my fish. He's gotten away. He's gone. My brother screams in the next room. At first I think it's the fish and I quickly pull my hand out of the tank. My family, along with my aunt and uncle come out of the bedroom. My brother smells of ointment. His neck looks smooth and oily and redder than ever.

"Your hand is wet," he says to me. "Why is your hand wet?"

Yes, my hand is dripping water now onto my aunt's threadbare carpeting. My uncle looks at my hand as if trying to decide what kind of ointment it might need.

"I dropped something in the toilet," I say, "and I had to reach in and get it. When I say it I have this terrible sinking feeling like I've been caught with my pants down, that the fish and I both have been caught with our pants down. No one seems satisfied with the explanation but at the moment at least they seem willing to drop it.

"Let's go," my mother says. "We've had enough excitement for one night."

8:30-We all pile back in the car. My journey is over. How do I feel? Disappointed. Frustrated. Itchy. I probably caught my brother's rash. But what else is new?

11 P.M.–7 A.M.-Last night I dream that I have become the very fish I want to touch, that I live in a giant fish tank in a Chinese restaurant, and that, unlike most fish, I keep a journal.

Journal of the Fish:

What the hell was that? I know what death is. It's when some waiter swoops you up in a net and removes you from the tank. That's called death or what's known around here as the big frying pan in the kitchen. That's fine. I've learned to expect that. That's just the natural end of things.

But this? I can't start thinking about this now. I'll go crazy. Off the deep end. I'm already bumping into the sides of the tank. I didn't even know there were sides to the tank. A little carp is eying me, at every turn. Never a reason.

Just do it. Path, view, city, to the city, getting seasick, now when did I ever get seasick? It was a hand, clearly a hand, you go through life moving always in a certain direction never expecting a hand in the tank, a net yes, but a hand, ouch, bump, one more like that and I'm damaged goods, cut up and thrown to the cats.

Can barely see now, darkness, darkness, once I was a fish swimming in pure fishness as in a dream until the waiter came to get me but none of us know just when that is, except the busier it gets at the restaurant the more likely…most of us wait paralyzed with fear, that's no way to live-some die of old age or are destroyed for that smell, the smell that comes from worry and anxiety. Worrying makes you unspeakably dry and tasteless and most of all you stink—the cats scream in excitement—some sexual thing—blood freezes—the little human fingers moving—pain pain there is no end only beginnings—glub glub—phit phit phit—swoosh swoosh swoosh—motionless unraveled—my eyes turn inward and I see the unfathomable nonsense of fish guts—I must go on, however. End of journal. End of dream.

9:30—We're on our way home. My mother warns my father about red lights. Then my father says something that stuns me. He turns to my mother. I see his profile. His shadow. He seems a great man now, the man who pilots my journey, who is all powerful, able to drive magnificently in and around traffic, cut off the unsuspecting, outsmart and out maneuver those who are on to him and at the same time be able to turn to my mother to speak.

I listen carefully as he begins to open his mouth, not very wide, my father does not open his mouth wide ever; he grinds his teeth and that is where all his power and weakness lies. Chicken bones don't have a chance with him but neither do his teeth with chicken bones. So he turns to my mother and I'm all ears because whatever he says affects my life no matter how ridiculous it may be and he says,

"You know I think we should get a fish tank."

I should be thrilled but yet my stomach sinks; I get that feeling that something important, like my heart, has been sucked out of me. But I'm thinking, shouldn't I be happy? My God I could get fish, all the fish I wanted and touch them all day. But something is wrong. For the first time my mother's words become a comfort to me, offer me hope.

"Fish tank," she says. "Are you out of your mind? That's all we need," she says to my father.

This shuts my father up. I think he expects me to say something in his defense like I want it too, to start whining in his defense like "Why not? I'd take care of it. I'd change the water. I'd feed the fish. I'd throw out the dead ones. Pleeeese!" But instead I say nothing.

"Is he going to clean up the mess?" I suddenly hear my mother ask.

"All right," my father says. "All right." He has already given up. Thank God my father gives up so easily.

Now there is just silence. Just darkness and silence and I think of the fish again in my aunt's tank circling and circling forever, the smell of ointment, the beautiful Middle Village sunsets and in my head I'm trying to touch him and each time I miss, just miss, the orange fish with the brown stripes who must think of me too, waiting constantly for my return.

"When are we going back?" I ask my mother. "When are we going back to Middle Village?"

"Not so fast," she says. "Not so fast," she says as my father passes another red light.

We wait again for the sirens, but nothing comes.

"Can I get fish?" I ask again. The relief of a sirenless world weighs heavily upon us. "Phht, phht," I say. "Swoosh, swoosh."

My mother looks at me, strangely. She begins to rub my arm, as if she is trying to rub something off of it.

"It's the ointment," my brother says. "He put some of the ointment on himself and he doesn't even have a rash."

But that's not it. I can tell what my mother is thinking.

"Swoosh, swoosh," I say again. "Phit phit. Glib glib."

Then she starts to touch me again, my arms, my neck, my forehead.

"What a moron," my brother says.

But not my mother. My mother is thinking real hard about something. My mother is smarter than that, I think to myself as another red light fades into the distance.

DYSPNEA

From the first day I knew her, she had trouble breathing. "I...like...you...a...lot," she once said to me and then was completely out of breath. What was funny was she came from a long line of long-winded people, people who barely took a breath between words, who spat and drooled rather than hold back a single word. They were people suspicious of other people who took deep breaths. Needless to say, Dyspnea was a problem for them, not to mention a constant embarrassment.

"Spit it out, already!" her father would shout at her, but instead she just choked on whatever it was she was trying to say or swallow.

They took her to doctors but the doctors only gave her pills that made her breath easier, not faster. Then one day she was in a car with her brother Ted who was driving and at one point during the ride she said, "Ted...we...are... going....to...be...killed!" But by the time she said it, he was already dead.

She, however, lived. To regret it, of course. She told me this. Slowly and deliberately, she told me this. She saw it coming all right, saw the car coming right at them which for some reason, Ted never saw. But her family never once blamed Ted's vision, only Dyspnea's breathing. After that, they hated her. Ted had been drinking she wanted to tell them. Ted drove like a maniac even when he was sober. Ted wanted to crash. Ted wanted to kill both of us she wanted to tell them, but it just wouldn't come out. First, she needed a receptive audience. People who really wanted to know the truth. Next, she needed the space. A good physical distance between her and them, just enough to have enough oxygen to say everything she had to say because most of the time they took away what little breath she had and sucked up what little oxygen there was in the room. And most of all, she needed silence. As much silence as she needed, she had to have. And this was something they just wouldn't give her.

She was just a girl and she knew that was a disadvantage. This too was connected to her weakness. Ted, who was a boy, never had trouble breathing. If anything, he breathed too well. He got all the breath they'd say, and she got all the looks. But looks weren't enough. In fact, they were very bad. She seemed to them like a defective doll with a run down battery that wasn't worth replacing. Girls liked silence. That's what they thought.

"I hate silence," her father told her once. "It shows weakness and deceit. It's left-wing and atheistic. It makes my skin crawl."

And while she was trying to collect enough air in her lungs to disagree, Ted said, "You know what, Dad?"

"What son?" his father asked him in a kind of deathly anti-silent roar.

"Whenever I'm with a girl and she doesn't say anything I feel like I'm being castrated."

The father laughed and Dyspnea thought she had finally caught enough air to scream, but all she could manage was a long, painful hiss like a punctured tire. The mother, probably at the end of her rope by now, turned to her and said, "If you don't start breathing, no supper!" So she was forced back into her room where she practiced breathing in front of a mirror.

For the most part, Dyspnea and I have good times together. I don't mind the silence, not really. Sometimes we sit in the park and all I hear are the birds chirping, the leaves rustling, and the measured railing of Dyspnea's breath.

"Just don't think about it," I tell her. "I don't, and it just comes naturally."

And then she looks at me as if I too have betrayed her and she says, "If...I...don't...think...about...it...I'll...die."

And she would too. How quickly those of us who can breathe forget. When I take Dyspnea into my arms, I feel her resisting me, struggling with all her strength to push me away. I assume I have taken her breath away, but it's more than that. She looks at me as if I am just another man out to destroy her.

I leave her apartment and when I hit the night air, suddenly I too have trouble breathing. Sympathy breathing, I think. As I head into the subway, my wheezing grows worse until I can no longer separate its sound from the sound of the train heading towards me. It all seems so hopeless. Should I leap? Or perhaps just buy an inhaler. Why do anything rash? Why wait till things get worse? So many questions, and so little air to answer them with.

If there was one thing I always thought Dyspnea resented about me, it was my callous indifference towards my ability to breath. That's just the way it is, I told her, but nothing to her was the way it was. No one thinks about breathing, I explained to her, unless they really have to.

"That's just what's wrong with the world," she'd say. "And…if…you…really…loved…me…you'd…think…about…it," she added breathlessly.

I returned to her apartment the next day just oozing with oxygen. And that whole morning I read poetry to her, trying to match the slow rhythmical cadences of the poems with her own measured breaths. "Your breathing is like poetry," I told her, and she liked that.

Dyspnea is good for me. She has slowed down my life which I have needed. She has made me think about things now before I do them. There are many past threats I have not gone through with. I have not quit my job. I have not pursued the waitress who keeps giving me looks at the diner. No, instead I have lain with the deep rasping silences of Dyspnea's breathing and I have found peace there.

On Thanksgiving Day, we went to Dyspnea's parents' house. Her father carved the turkey and looked at Dyspnea the whole time he did it. Nowhere on his face was the look of forgiveness. Ted being dead there was not much in her father's mind to be thankful for. Her mother put some stuffing and cranberry sauce on a plate and placed it in front of where Ted would have been sitting. There were no turnips on the plate. "Ted doesn't like turnips," her mother said as if Ted were still alive and had stepped out for a moment. There was complete silence during the meal except for Dyspnea's treacherous breathing. What had comforted me before, now frightened me as if each of her breaths were the ticks of a time bomb.

Something terrible was going to happen tonight, I thought to myself, as her mother went off to get the dessert. It was pumpkin pie, my favorite. Ted's still full plate was taken away and piled up with the rest of the dishes.

"He eats so little these days," Ted's mother said. "And believe me, it's starting to show," she added.

"The kids got a lot on his mind!" Ted's father yelled at her.

Obviously, they had both gone mad. Barely having touched my pie, I got up from the table without being noticed and headed for the bathroom. I could not touch the pie. It seemed to me now a pie of death, as if it had been sliced and served by and for the dead. It even smelled like death and from that day forward I was never able to look at pumpkin pie quite the same way again.

On the way to the bathroom, I turned into Ted's room instead. It looked again like he was not dead but had merely stepped out for a moment. His bed was not made. His TV was on, playing a tape of extreme car racing, but at such a low volume one could barely hear the sound of the crashing. On the night table near his bed, there was a photo of a high school football team and I recognized Ted from other photos I had seen around the house that night and in the photo he was the one not wearing a helmet. On the wall over his bed was a calendar of naked women stuck on September five years ago the month Ted was killed, and I imagined it would be stuck that way for a long time to come, perhaps long after those naked women were dead. I wondered what these women would think about being so immortalized, to be lusted after by the living and haunted by the dead. There were other photos of women as well, in various stages of dress and undress, but there was no indication of whom they were. His various conquests, I imagined.

What was it like to be Ted, I wondered, so I got out of my clothes, inserted myself beneath the rumpled covers of the bed and proceeded to watch extreme car racing. Just then his mother walked in.

"Go to sleep now, Teddy. It's very late," she said. "And please, Teddy," she added. "Lower that TV. We can hear it all the way at the end of the house."

I said nothing. Besides, I couldn't make it any lower if I tried. Then, of course, there was his father popping his head into the room.

"Look, son," he said, loud enough to hear him all the way at the end of the house, "you stay up as long as you like, and if you do have a girl under the bed, more power to you. Your mother's a light sleeper; otherwise, I'd come in and join you."

"Sure, Dad," I told him. "Maybe next time. We share everything, don't we?"

Then the father laughed, this terrible, devious laugh as if we shared some terrible secret together.

I no longer felt now that I should get dressed and take Dyspnea home, but for some reason felt stuck here, as if it were here that I belonged. Suddenly, this had all become mine: The room, the bed, the car racing video, the calendar of naked women, the photos on the wall, the mother, the father, Ted's nakedness, and even the imaginary girl whom I swear I could hear breathing quite normally under the bed.

And then, of course, she came in. Even in the darkness, especially in the darkness I knew it was her. After all, I recognized the breathing. No one else could breath as loudly and as lovely as Dyspnea. She was coming to me. She wanted me.

"Please," she said. And then I waited as her wheezing blended into the soft distant undertones of a car wreck.

"Please...don't," she pleaded.

"Why not?" I asked in a voice that I did not recognize but which very well could have been Ted's and she said, "come," and then she said, "into," and then she said, "my," and then "room," and finally "tonight," and then I put it all together—"Please—don't—come—into—my—room—tonight."

And then I said, "And if I do?" Just like Ted would have said, and she said, "I'll...scream....I'll...scream."

But she couldn't scream. Ted knew and I knew she couldn't scream, and yet she felt compelled, night after night, that Ted had been coming into her room, to warn him, a warning he no doubt laughed at, so I too began to laugh, to laugh uncontrollably like Ted must have done.

But she just stood there and with all the breath she could manage, she kept repeating, "I'll...scream....I'll...scream," and then I heard her breathing begin to move away, to fade into the distance, and I knew what Ted would do next. I knew everything. I knew that she never tried to warn Ted at all in the car that night, but instead had grabbed the wheel herself and steered it into the oncoming traffic, so that she and Ted might both die, and her parents would have to spend the rest of their lives together, alone.

So now, knowing everything, I got out of bed, put my clothes back on, turned off the TV, ripped the calendar off the wall, and threw all the photos of the women I felt too ashamed to look at into the garbage can at the side of the bed. Yes, I thought. We would go right home now and work on Dyspnea's screaming.

THE HOMELESS

On the way to my dentist, I saw two homeless men dressed in green baggy pants, woolen caps, one green, one blue, big floppy black shoes with the laces untied, one following the other, closely, one practically on the other's heels, so the one in front, the one being followed, would turn around from time to time and scream at the one following him, "Quit following me," he'd scream, "or I'll kill you!" But the one following him, the one in the blue cap kept insisting to the other one, the one he was following, that he was not following him, that it was his imagination, that he was paranoid, that he, the follower, had just as much right to walk on the street as he, the one being followed did.

And then they'd walk a few more feet, the one following the one in front of him practically walking in his shoes and the guy in front screaming, but without turning around, "You stop following me or I'll cut your throat, you hear me?" And then the other guy would say, "Who the fuck's following you, man? You got a complex or somethin'? How important do you think you are? If I was really followin' you, you'd know I was followin' you because I'd be right up your mean ass if I was."

And it would go on like this for a while, the one being followed yelling back at the one following him, the one following him yelling back even louder, practically in his ear that he wasn't following him at all, not even close, that they were so far apart they might as well have been in different countries he was so far from following him.

And this went on for a while longer until the one being followed stopped in front of a bank like he was going to take out some money, but what he was there for was to keep the door open for people coming in to use the ATM machines.

He'd say things like "Good morning, ladies, homeless, homeless, good morning gentlemen, homeless, homeless,"sticking out his cup instead of his hand as if he were a candidate running for public office, so once in a while he'd get some change from people walking out, but mostly people seemed afraid of him, thinking perhaps he'd rob them or follow them home. The guy who had been following him seemed to have disappeared, but when the one who had been followed began to walk in the street again, there he was, the follower, appearing out of nowhere it seemed, right behind him, on his heels, whispering now into the guy he was following's ear and the guy who was being followed did seem to listen, slowing down even to catch what the other was saying and then he began to turn red and then redder and then even redder and then to shake his fist in the air.

What could the one who was following the one being followed possibly have to say to him that he couldn't just scream out in the street for all to hear and besides, I thought, what could be worse than being homeless? Soon the guy being followed started to speed up again and the guy who was following him, who had been whispering something in his ear so bad that it was worse than being homeless, started to shout just like I thought he should be doing all along. "Hey, man!" he shouted after him. "Hey, man those are just the facts and if you can't face the facts then you ain't a man." Then the other one said, still not turning around, "I know one fact man and that's that you are my worst nightmare!"

These two men did not work well together. There was tension between them. You could tell that just by looking at them. There seemed to be this hellish expression on their faces, much like on my own, though mine was dental related, whereas theirs seemed to come from a longstanding saga of profound disgust and disappointment; perhaps in each other. Yes, perhaps they knew each other after all, knew each other so well there was no limit to the hate that each could harbor for the other in each of their hearts, the hate reserved only for those who have loved each other once but have had some sort of falling out.

As for me, I was really in a lot of pain and didn't want to miss my dentist appointment, but this was interesting. Watching these men was important for me because it helped me stay focused, helped me concentrate on the small details of things as well as the big ones. I needed that. My life had become vague and uncertain. I was forgetting people's names and they were forgetting mine. Even the dentist kept calling me a different name which made me think it was someone else's root canal he was doing. The world was becoming a terrifying place. At least these homeless men had focus, purpose, one who must always follow, the other who must always be followed.

So I continued to watch them how after a while they both started to speed up, then to slow down again to find the right pace, the right pace for them, for the one who followed and the one being followed. Once in a while one would say to the other, "You're imagining things man. You've got one sick overactive imagination!" Sometimes they would say such hideous things to each other, far worse than I would ever have said to my wife or she to me, far worse than I would even expect men without homes to say to each other.

This went on for several more blocks until they came to a crossroads. Actually, it was my own crossroads, 71st and Lexington, where I'd have to make my turn west towards Madison, the moment I had to decide whether or not to turn away from them and follow the path to my dentist's office. Indeed, despite the fact that I myself had a home, a job, a wife, a son, was a member of the New York Health and Racquet club, not to mention a Republican, I was becoming obsessed with these men.

But then something happened which seemed to make my decision for me, because I knew then that the moment the one in front had suddenly slowed down, had actually caused the one behind him to stumble, to practically fall over him, that a major turning point had taken place, that this relationship had moved on to another plane entirely. I was excited, and when suddenly one of them, I could not tell who, took a swing at the other one's head, I became elated.

Elation does not come easy with me. I had many moments in my life when to all the world it appeared that I should have been elated about something but I wasn't. This would include my marriage, my job, the birth of my son, the election of George W. Bush, but I just wasn't. But now, with one swing of a man's arm, I felt an elation I never felt before. It wasn't like caffeine or cocaine or sex or anything like that, no quick fix, but a kind of release like finally tackling a problem that's been nagging you for years, grabbing it by the neck you might say and then squeezing the life out of it.

It's funny. I was thinking about myself so much I lost track of the two men and if not for the fact that they had stopped to fight each other, I may have lost sight of them completely. They were on the ground now wrestling with each other. Certainly no love lost here, I thought, although still there seemed a familiarity between them, as if they had done this before, a kind of blind grabbing of shoulders and bones and ribs like two lovers who know where each other's erogenous zones are without looking.

For example, now that their caps were off, I noticed that one was bald and that the other had hair, and again, without looking, the one who was bald pulled the other one's hair, just until he winced, as if he knew exactly how hard and how long to pull to get him to wince just to know, to get a sense of what was to follow. Then the one with the hair dug his fingernails into an indentation between the other man's neck and the back of his skull as if he knew the exact measure, the very depth and breadth of that indentation. At this point, I no longer knew who was who, whether it was the one who was being followed who had the upper hand or else the one who had followed him.

It wasn't until the one who was being followed was finally on top of the other one, his knee in his groin, his hands around the prone man's neck, that I recognized him. Yes, I would know that man anywhere, the victim, the harassee, the keeper of bank doors. He was bald, completely bald and had scars along the border between his neck and the back of his skull to prove it. Yes, this was my man. If he were a broken racehorse I still would have bet on him. I began to think of this man as my mouth and the one who followed him, the one with the hair, as the disease that ravaged it.

It was clear to me now that I was taking sides. As long as the one who was being followed was on top of the one who followed him, my pain was gone, but as soon as the other had the upper hand again, my pain returned which proved to me once again that evil always triumphed over good.

In fact, I remembered quite clearly now it was the day I had an intestinal flu and came home early from work that I found my wife in bed with our next door neighbor, a liberal democrat, and I just walked away and never said a word about it but just went into our neighbor's garden and broke the nozzle off his garden hose. Then there was the day I had a sudden outbreak of eczema and went down to the basement for some ointment when I found my son doing drugs and how could I ever forget the terrible case of pink eye I contracted just days before the other vice-presidents in my company pulled the rug out from under me, stole my downsizing ideas and, after careful study, decided to get rid of me.

So even though I was a man who didn't care much about anyone and said very little about anything, I suddenly found myself cheering out loud. "Kill him! Kill him!" I shouted when the hairless man was on top. And when the bald one was on the bottom again, I'd shout, "Don't be killed! Please don't be killed!" And then, for a long time, just when it seemed to the whole world that these two would go on like this forever, that they might very well die from the exhaustion of the struggle itself, my man, the one with the indentation in the back of his neck, finally, as if to prove that in the long run determination and hard work can pay off, that there is no yoke so heavy that it can not be crushed, had his hands so firmly gripped around the other one's neck, that the other one, the one with the hair, could no longer move.

Then, the other one, the one who's neck was so firmly gripped by the other, yet apparently not gripped hard enough so that he could not speak, as if he, the one who had been followed, wanted him to say something, wanted him to start begging for his life, began to beg not for his life, but for his death, or at least to indicate that death would not be the worst thing in the world.

"Go ahead and kill me!" he told the man whose fingers gripped his neck, "Go ahead and kill me. What have I got to live for anyway?" This reminded me of the time I had my hands around my wife's neck and she said the same thing. "Go ahead and kill me! What have I got to live for, anyway?" And my son, who said, while I had my hands around his neck, "Go ahead, Dad. You'd be doing me a favor." Funny how I always thought I was the one who had nothing to live for.

Then I noticed how the man on top, the one who had it all under control now, started to loosen his fingers from the other man's neck and then to remove them from his neck entirely, and then I saw that terrible, strained look on his face, the one that had been about to strangle the other, begin to disappear and then he seemed more relaxed than I had ever seen him look. Then, just as the other one, the one with the hair, the one who had nearly been strangled by the other, got up to begin following the other one, the bald one, again, a cop, who seemed to come out of nowhere, grabbed him, struggled with him a bit, and then dragged him into his patrol car.

"No!" cried a hot dog man from the corner who had been observing me suspiciously as if rather than being the kind of man who would buy a hot dog I was more the kind of man who might destroy the whole hot dog business.

"You have the wrong man!" he suddenly cried out, pointing his finger at me.

But it was too late. The man who once followed the other, the man who in all this distraction had left his blue cap behind, was gone, and the other man, the holder of bank doors, just stood there now, crying, not moving a muscle, looking like he had just lost his best friend. Then, much to my surprise, I too started to cry. I too began to feel the pain, not of a bad tooth so much, but of loss, of abandonment, of that vast cavity of unfulfilled desire, so I pulled my shirt just a little bit out of my pants, untied my shoelaces, put the blue cap on my head that used to belong to the man who had been taken away, and when the other man, my man, the exact measure, the very depth and breadth of whose skull I wanted to know better, started to move, I followed him.

PLACENTA

This was a week for dreams. Martha dreamed that Felix's father died and then two weeks later, Felix himself was dead. Mike's mother dreamed that Mike's play had been produced on Broadway and that at the cast party afterwards he denied his mother, had her credentials checked, and only after the supplication of certain family members whom he did not recognize, did he finally relent and allow her to sit at a small non-VIP table near the men's room. As it turned out, Mike's play was not produced, anywhere, and still, because a dream to his mother was as real as reality itself, perhaps even more real, he had a lot of explaining to do. Two weeks later, Mike did publish a short story, old, nearly forgotten, that is he forgot he ever wrote it, which was published in some obscure British Columbian publication. "I told you," his mother said, but still he didn't see the connection between her dream about getting a play on Broadway and his story getting published in some obscure journal in Canada. As usual, his mother had over-dreamed for him, had over-believed in him, while he never dreamed at all, while he only considered himself a failure.

Dreams, other people's in particular, were starting to get on Mike's nerves. He always said how can you care about things that don't really happen, that have no connection to real life. Then why should we care about your writing, they told him since it was all made up anyway, so he decided to listen to their dreams and then, after a while, he even decided to steal them. Then his stories began to sound like other people's dreams and lost their footing in reality and people, except his mother, urged him to write like he used to because they could get as much out of sleeping now as they could out of his stories. So they struck a deal. You don't tell me your dreams and I don't write about them. What else could he do? These people dreamed like crazy. They have far more dreams than I have stories, he thought. This is because they don't have to work at it. It just happens, like putting the TV on. But if I put the TV on, Mike thought, it's just a blank screen. He wished he could sit in front of a blank screen and some story would suddenly take form, but it never happened. Most people dreamed about their fears and frustrations. Mike wrote about them. He had to make sense out of them. He had to create other people, people who never or only partially existed before. He had to write one sentence after another until he came up with just the right kind of revelation about life to satisfy his readers. And he had to do it in a kind of subtle, sometimes underhanded way, so the reader wouldn't know, no, wouldn't feel, intuit, suspect what was happening until it actually happened.

And what if he couldn't think of one? Revelations were not easy to come by. His mind was not a container of revelations nor did they come unsolicited and just swim across his brain like so many tropical fish. Often, he'd work backwards. He'd look for revelations first. Everywhere he went, he tried to find the truth behind things. If a light went out suddenly on a deserted street he would not see it merely as a burnt out light bulb, but as some greater truth, a metaphor perhaps for the unpredictability of life or the transitory nature of the soul. Deep down he knew it only meant the unpredictability of street lamps or the transitory nature of light bulbs, but he couldn't let himself think that way or he'd be doomed as a writer.

And what about love? How did love fit into all this? He was finding it increasingly difficult, no, impossible, to write about love anymore. People dreamt about it all the time. Recently, he dreamt he was on a date with a woman he could not recognize. He and the woman were walking on a deserted street when suddenly the street lights went out. Darkness enveloped both the street and his dream. He felt he was suffocating. When the lights finally came on again, the woman was gone and his friend Martin was there instead. Perhaps the woman had turned into his friend Martin since the one thing he could remember, even days later, was that they were both wearing the same orange blouse. When he told Martin the dream, he left out the part about the blouse but did mention the walk along the deserted street, the lights suddenly going out and how when they came back on again, it was he, Martin, standing there instead of the woman. This seemed to disturb Martin. "Why would I be standing there instead of the woman?" he asked Mike. "It was a dream," Mike told him. "How should I know?" But Martin wasn't happy. The dream seemed to affect him more than it did Mike. Imagine, Mike thought, if I had told him about the orange blouse.

Later that week, Martin told him about his own dream, that he too was walking with a woman down a deserted street, a woman he recognized quite well, a woman he knew once, whom he knew very well, very, very well, he said, while he was living in California. Mike was jealous. Mike had dreamt once that Martin was living in California but couldn't recall if he ever knew he really did. And what of the woman? Was he just saying that to make him jealous? He didn't know. "And you," his friend said to him. "Me?" he asked. "Yes, you were in the dream too." "How? Where?" he asked his friend. "In the background," Martin told him. "You were watching us and taking notes." "Oh," he said, but really this didn't surprise him. At least he was there, lurking somewhere in the shadows of their unconscious. He knew this was the way almost everyone thought of him, in or out of their dreams. He just did not insinuate himself enough into their every day fears or anxieties about the very volatile and unpredictable nature of love. Just as in his writing, he needed to impart a truth about something, about himself really, in order to have a firmer basis from which to dream about it and for others to dream about him. There were things he could only know through the imagination but that was not enough because they needed to come through that part of him that was always empty and from which great revelations emerge. Basically, he couldn't think of anyone who would love him and he couldn't think of any reason why they should.

So he sat among the clutter of loveless stories he had written over the years and tried to remember the last time he, and not one of his characters, had been in love. But, alas, he couldn't remember. Other things got in the way. Books, movies, other people's dreams and stories, his own fantasies; perhaps even if he remembered, it might never have really happened. No, he had to admit to himself that the well was dry and so his empty spot continued to ache through all his dreamless nights.

Then came the morning his friend Martin called him. "Mike," he said. "Do you remember that girl you met in college, what's her name, the funny name, you know the one with that ridiculous name?" "I don't remember," Mike told him. "Sure you do," Martin insisted. "It started with a "P." Projecta, Pregenta, Protecta, something like that." Mike felt something rush out of him as if he had been dropped blindfolded out of a ten story window.

"Placenta?" he asked, bracing himself for the inevitable, painful confirmation. "That's it!" Mike shouted. He hated that meaningless enthusiasm Martin always showed about things that were absolutely none of his business. "It sounded like she was pregnant all the time," Martin added and Mike remembered thinking the same thing himself, as if life always moved inside her. He remembered the time she let him kiss her, out of pity perhaps or his own relentless pleading so that if she didn't let him he'd do something drastic, not to her, but to himself. And when he did kiss her, he remembered how he tried to push himself inside her, not just part of himself, for some temporal pleasure, but all of himself, to actually get himself inside her, to lie peacefully, quietly, just along the inside of her stomach wall. He knew, even at the time, he knew how strange this was, but that's how he felt. So yes, he supposed he had loved once, though in a strange way, in a way he could not express to others, not even to himself.

When he told Placenta his desire, she became frightened and pushed him away. She misunderstood his desire, so he thought what good were desires at all if they were always misunderstood, if they were always dismissed or twisted or shoved off into some feckless, craving part of his brain. He remembered he didn't see her much after that and how ashamed he felt being unable to express his feelings for women in a normal way like some other men could. Perhaps he had loved too much or not enough but either way he decided never to love again.

"What about her?" he asked his friend Martin.

"I had a dream about her last night," he said, "and you were in it."

"Watching? Taking notes?" he asked, bracing himself once again for the inevitable, painful confirmation.

"Not at all," Martin told him. "You were right there. The whole time. I just wish I could remember what you said."

Mike wanted to dismiss this right away. He wanted to tell his friend that he couldn't care less, that dreams, especially Martin's dreams, were meaningless and empty, but he couldn't get himself to believe this any more. He was excited, more excited than he had been in years, maybe ever. He wanted to believe now that Martin's dream was as real as the voice telling him about it over the phone. "Where was she?" he asked Martin as if he were certain she were waiting for him someplace at that very moment, perhaps somewhere within the convolutions of his friend's brain.

"It seemed," his friend said. "It seemed it may have been around the college. Maybe in the cafeteria."

"Seemed?" Mike asked. "Don't you know? It's your own dream for godsakes!"

"That's just it," Martin said. "It's a dream. Everything seems rather than is."

Mike was angry. "Then why bother telling me about it, about her, if you don't know?"

"I thought you might like to know," Martin said. "I know you liked her."

"Then why?" Mike asked. And he really meant this with all his being. "Then why are you dreaming about her and not me dreaming about her?"

"You know I can't answer that, Mike." Martin told him. "I wish I could, but you know I can't." But really, how much did he know? Maybe he wasn't really talking to Martin now about Martin's dream about Placenta, but only dreaming he was. Nevertheless, he was angry. "What were we doing in the cafeteria?" Mike asked, although he really wanted to say, "What were you doing in the cafeteria?" He started to believe his friend was cheating on him. Who knew about dreams? After all, there was no guarantee it was actually Mike Martin was dreaming about. Didn't he read once that everyone in your dreams is really you so that in this case Mike wouldn't be Mike at all, but would really be Martin? It was all too confusing, too unpredictable, but still there was always a chance…

"I believe," Martin went on to say, "if you were indeed in the cafeteria, then you were probably sitting at a table." He knew Martin was goading him with this vagueness, but vagueness was okay with Mike. He liked vagueness. It gave him some room to maneuver, to avoid those unrelenting, in your face details that always pinned you down like a helpless insect.

"And where were you?" Mike asked.

"I don't know," Martin said. "Observing you, I guess, from the convolutions of my brain."

"And was it both of us?" Mike asked. "Were we both sitting at the table? Placenta and me? Me and Placenta?" He loved saying her name. He couldn't believe he had gone all these years without saying it. He wouldn't, he thought, make that mistake again.

"Yes," Martin informed him. "The two of you were sitting at a table and you were showing her something."

"Something?"

"Yes," Martin said. "It looked like you were holding something up to the light, like photographs."

"Photographs?" Mike asked.

"Yes, photographs. And when you showed her the last one, suddenly, though I could be wrong, she stood up and was…naked."

"Naked!" Mike exclaimed. He felt betrayed. All along he really didn't want to think of this as a dream and now it was beginning to sound too much like one, like some ludicrous dream hatched from his friend's unspectacular, yet often lewd, brain.

"Yes, I believe that to be the case," Martin said. "At least I think so. And then, if memory does not escape me, you stood up too and she grabbed you and pulled you towards her and then..."

"And then what?"

"And then...you kind of disappeared. At least you weren't there in the dream anymore." Mike knew why he disappeared. At least he hoped he knew and hoped he knew exactly where he disappeared to.

"Fine," Mike said. "Is there anything else you think I should know?"

"Know?" Martin asked. "Know about what?"

"Nothing," Mike said. Then he said "Nothing" again like it meant something.

"Well," Martin said. "I just wanted you to know, that's all."

"Know what?" Mike asked.

"Nothing," Martin said. "Just know."

"Okay, now I know."

"Good."

"Yeah, thanks," Mike said.

"For what?" Martin asked.

"For having my dream. As you know I've been having some trouble lately..."

"Yes, Martin said. "I know."

The next day, Mike visited the college cafeteria. He looked around but recognized no one. This was a good sign, he thought, a good sign that he was not dreaming and seeing people he knew or once knew who shouldn't have been there at all, so that he felt he was really there, in some strange place, years later. And now everyone was on a cell phone and though they were all disconnected from life around them, listening to some droning, disembodied voice, still it seemed to him they were connected at least to the illusion of something real, like love, and whether in its throes or its denial, still it had something to do with love, the idea of love, which Martin had nothing to do with whether on the phone or in person. Then, as if in a dream, he saw her. It was Placenta. He could tell by the life that moved inside her. He walked up to her and said, "Placenta," and she looked right through him, the way people might in dreams, and said, "I must be dreaming." "No," he said. "It's me who's dreaming." "Well," she said, "one of us must be." He knew she was right but he just didn't know which one of them it was. He wished Martin was here so that he could tell him, tell him what seemed to be and what actually was.

"I have the photos," he said.

"Photos?" she asked. "What photos?" Her question surprised him. Maybe, he thought, it was her dream, after all.

"Of us," he said.

"Really," she said. "And when were these taken?"

"When we were in love," he said.

"In love?" she asked. "Us? I don't recall…"

"Don't you remember?" he interrupted, "how you used to let me lie within the walls of your stomach?" He could hear now the urgent clattering of dishes and silverware in the background as if something were coming to an end and that he would have to leave soon.

"You must have the wrong stomach," she said. "I don't recall any such thing. In fact, I barely recall you."

"Then why are you here?" he asked.

"I'm taking a course in Real Estate." Something must be wrong, he thought. This was the same cafeteria, wasn't it? She was the same Placenta, wasn't she? Yet, despite all this, nothing was going the way he expected it to go.

"Look," he said to her. "Look!" And he held out his photos to her, photos that had sat in his desk drawer for years, except now he noticed they were not actually the photos at all, but the negatives of the photos, the bare, skeletal remains of all his dreams, of the very proof that he had once lain within the stomach wall of Placenta and the very means by which he might do so again.

"I can't see anything," she said.

"Hold them up to the light!" Mike pleaded. "Hold them up to the light!"

"I won't!" she said, looking not quite through him this time.

"I could still send them out to be developed," he said, but he knew it was too late. He knew there wasn't a photo lab in the world that could save him now.

"Excuse me," she said. "I have to go. I have to go pick up my kids."

So now she was Mrs. Placenta, he thought, and he felt sad that others had already occupied the space inside her.

"But what about us?" he asked. What about our dreams?"

"What dreams?" she asked, looking right at him this time as people often do in reality. Then she began to laugh, and she laughed and laughed and when she laughed it seemed to him that the life that once moved inside her had become stillborn. He could sense now that something had changed. He was disappointed. Perhaps he could start over again. Maybe he could go out and come back as many times as he had to in order to make sure it all worked out the way it was supposed to. But how was it supposed to work out? No, he knew he would have to forget Placenta now. Obviously, they had grown apart and now, rather than lie inside of her, he would write about her instead, for he felt certain that out of the ashes of dead dreams revelation is born.

THE BAGEL KING

For some reason the nights have turned ugly here. It's the neighborhood. Once it was peaceful. I used to enjoy staring at the street lamps where moths, perhaps the most silent creatures on Earth used to chase each other around them, but now I don't dare go near the window. There are people out there who aim for anything that moves against a lighted background. And forget about sleep. Sleep is for those forty exists down the highway, deep in the wooded suburbs where dogs howl like wolves to keep the burglars away. I used to get a good seven or eight hours of sleep, but now it's two—maybe three—depending on the length of the car alarm or if I can get the screaming to become part of my dreams, dreams of ghastly murders or of filthy blind love creeping along the dark alleys of my building. It's the morning I look forward to the brand new bagel store just down the block and that beautiful young girl behind the counter.

It was a remarkably clean bright place, especially for the neighborhood, and there was a long counter in the back where you could sit and eat your bagel and drink your coffee and look at yourself in the mirror, and I could always see how calm I looked and how happy I was to be there. When I bought my bagel from the young girl, I always eyed her carefully to see if she was into me in any way. I always paid with big bills so there'd be a lot of change, and I could watch her tongue swing like a metronome as she tried to figure out the change. Then I'd watch how softly she poured the money into my hands which longed to caress her. Don't get me wrong. It was the bagels, too. I needed bagels. Perhaps even more than young girls, I needed bagels because chances are perhaps if the girl behind the counter was a woman around my own age I would still come here. As for myself, I was not a young man, at least not a boy. Let's say I was not quite as old as the young girl was young, and I doubt she suspected half of what I thought about her as she sliced my bagel.

But yes, even more than her, if you can believe it, I needed bagels. When I woke up every morning I did not need toast, bread, rolls, bialys, danishes, doughnuts, crullers or croissants. I needed a bagel. What it was about bagels, I wondered. Well, yes, now I couldn't think about my morning bagel without thinking about the girl, too, the way she stretched out her body sometimes like a dancer to get the unsalted ones way up on the top shelf. This wasn't my doing nor hers but the big sweaty guy in the back who was her boss. Yes, I needed bagels but sometimes I wondered whether or not the bagels just acted as a vehicle for what I really wanted, for what I really needed, which was the girl.

Don't laugh. After all, wasn't it was my obsession for young girls that had already set me back a few notches in life, that had denied me promotions and made every tenure at some public school or university a living hell?

Was it any wonder I often sought out food and in particular the solace of bagels and lox? Yes, lox, too. LOX. There was something about lox, the very word lox, the sight and smell of lox that made young girls nervous. They wanted no part of it. My mother had no problems with lox, my grandmother had no problems with lox, but my sister did. Once I asked the young girls of my class to write about it, but they refused. They insisted on another topic. The boys laughed like they knew something. There was one exception. There was one young girl who often baited me in front of the whole class daring me to go out with her some Sunday morning for bagels and lox. She specifically said LOX. BAGELS AND LOX. Just like that. When she read her assignment it was about a young girl who goes out with an older man, her professor in fact, for bagels and lox and eventually gets him entangled in a messy affair.

We went out. Her father was a crazed Vietnam veteran who threatened to cut my balls off, but I took my chances.

We went to the deli that served bagels rather than a bagel place that served deli. It was dark and dirty and the lox, as far as I could tell had the same coloring and texture as an old man's toupee. The girl screamed when it came to the table. I could see in her eyes that whatever had attracted her to me in the first place had diminished considerably. She forgot it was all my fault. I was like every other man, a liar, a cheater, a child molester, a renderer of bad lox. What right had I, she said, to be going out with someone young enough to be my daughter? I tried to calm her down, I kept sticking my fork into it, insisting it wouldn't move, that it was dead twice removed, that I had no idea it would arrive so badly damaged. All lox was not like this I assured her, just like all men were not like her father. Certainly, something must have happened back in the kitchen. I tried to tell her that we cannot always know what goes on in the kitchen. There are cheaters, deceivers.

"There's still a lot you don't know," I told her. "There's still a lot out there you have to learn."

"Oh, yeah?" she asked me. "And are you gonna be the one to teach me?"

I didn't answer her, but I looked at her as if I would be the one if she let me.

"Maybe you can meet my father one day," she said.

"I think he'd like that," I told her.

I brought the lox platter back to the counter. I thought this would impress her, teach her that when a person is not happy with something, she should put it right back into the face of the person who gave it to her. Lesson number one. But when I came back to the table, she was gone. There was a message scrawled on my napkin. "Lox Sucks and So Do You!" I believe it may have been written with the same pen she used to write about our messy but torrid affair. Lesson number two, I thought. You can't always predict good lox.

Yet, this bagel place was different. They always had good lox. I wish that girl could be with me right now, I thought, looking reminiscently at the wordless napkin before me.

But there was always the young girl behind the counter, I thought. I didn't think we'd ever speak until the first time she sliced lox for me. I didn't even know it was her first time until I saw her hands trembling over the cellophane. I got her through it, though. I told her to relax. It usually just handled itself I told her. I had never seen such fear in a girl's eyes. Twice she called for the big sweaty guy who turned out to be her father, but he was too busy.

"Look," I said. "You'll have to do it eventually. So, why not now? Why not do it for someone as patient and understanding as I am, someone that appreciates the slow, rigorous, painful road towards knowledge, rather than some lunatic who's double-parked out there?"

That was the most I ever said to her. After that she did fine, like she had been doing it all her life. So I said to her, "You'll see now how after this everything in life will be a breeze."

But then how was I to know the junkies would come to give her a hard time.

"I want some bagels and lox!" one of them screamed at her.

The fat greasy guy who turns out to be her father is somewhere way in the back in the dark factory part of the store up to his elbow in grease, wondering no doubt how he ever got into this mess, worrying about his daughter screwing things up in front.

She stares at them, a disdainful smirk on her face like this might chase them away.

"Hey, baby," another said in a rather exaggerated way, "how 'bout some BAY-GULLS and LOOOOXXXX!"

The external mocking tone of the lox haters, I think, who won't stop until they humiliate her or get her to turn over the day's proceeds.

"Joey here," one of them says, "can't live without bagels and lox. No sir, he's addicted to them!"

They all laugh at this, and I notice the various fluids spraying out of their mouths and noses ever so close to the lox which the girl recklessly left exposed on the counter, and at this point I just want out of the place.

The young girl tries to ignore them, but it's not easy. After all, they are practically in her face and she has to confront them like she would sour cream cheese or bad lox.

"Can I help you?" she asks them.

They laugh all over again. One of them pulls out a knife and sticks the sharp end of it against her throat. I stand up suddenly, but one of them pushes me back down. This indicates immediately that I'm no longer to harbor any thoughts of interfering. I look at the display case and notice the black eye of the white fish staring at me like it's my fault this guy's got a knife at her throat.

Then, while one holds a knife at the girl's throat and another stands over me making sure I don't get up, still another reaches over to the cash register. I think of saying something. I am a teacher, I thought, I have a way with words, so perhaps I could persuade these junkies to seek help. Or I can tell them I know what an addiction can be like for why else would I be here on a cold Sunday morning instead of in bed if not for the fact that I too was a kind of junkie?

I look over at the young girl and now of all times she is looking at me. Not with contempt but with pity as if she were sorry I had to be subjected to all this. I look back at her as if to say, perhaps when this is all over, we might…, but suddenly, to break the mood, a shot rings out, a bullet whizzes past our heads and there is the girl's father standing at the entrance way to the dark inner recess of the bagel factory with a rifle cradled in his arms. The junkie with the knife is smart not to cut the girl's throat but instead drops the knife on the counter.

The daughter points at me.

"He's okay," she tells her father and that big ugly mutant who has saved our lives looks over at me and recognizes right away a steady customer innocently caught up in crossfire.

"Yes, I'm okay," I tell him and, though I'm thrilled to see him, I'm nevertheless repulsed by the line of sweat running down the center of his shirt, by the wild tufts of hair sprouting from his chest, sprinkled with specks of sesame seeds and onion flakes as if he himself was some giant bagel come to life, another in a line of grotesque superheroes we must accept for their bravery and inner dignity rather than for their personal appearance.

He looks at me as if I'm not really okay, as if he knows the designs I might have on his daughter and so he would be just as pleased to shoot me as he would the junkies.

The girl looks at me with a look that says I should be quite pleased, as if her dad has shot more than one innocent bystander in the past.

"We're okay, too," one of the junkies says, looking at the girl, but the girl keeps quiet this time.

Then the junkie looks at me with painful black eyes like the whitefish as if to say, "You know how it is. You know what is like to be a junkie, right? But what can I do?"

I look to the girl for compassion, because, after all, she was the one with the knife at her throat and hope she will see it in her heart to save them. She looks back at me, as if to say, you know maybe when this is over we might..., and then her father, growing impatient, his bagels overboiling in the back, cocks his rifle and aims it straight at the junkie who once had a knife at his daughter's throat.

"Dad!" the girl cries.

He doesn't look at her.

"Oh, man," the junkie groans. "Oh, man."

"Dad, do you want to be cleaning up some bloody mess for the next two weeks or you want to sell bagels? Because after all Dad," she says proudly, "you are the Bagel King."

"Yes," he says matter-of-factly, looking at her now with the same scrutiny I thought I was only capable of, "I am the king of bagels."

He looks at the junkies as if to say this must be your lucky day, but despite this, they still cannot move but tremble in their shoes.

"Get out," he screams at them. "And if I ever catch you in here again, I'll blow your heads off!"

"Oh, man, Oh, man," one of the junkies says just before he leads all the others out of there.

"I thought they'd never leave," the girl says, turning to show me how unafraid she was.

But I can see her shaking and I know she won't be cutting bagels for awhile. The father has gone, one big hunk of solid shadow gone back to the darkness of his bagel factory. I look at the girl and realize now that her beauty only lives, her bagels only shine, her cream cheese only glows because somewhere back there where no light or sound can penetrate, the bagel king mixes together the ingredients that will save us all from a cruel and heartless world.

VIGO

The cock crowed too late. At least later than I would expect a cock to crow. We were headed for Vigo. I complained to the hotel manager about the cock and he promised to have it killed. Perhaps you could just reprimand it, I told him. Give it a good scolding, a good talking to. Remind it of the existence of automated wake-up calls. But he wouldn't hear of it. In his country, so he claimed, lateness in any capacity, by any species, was unpardonable and unforgivable. Yes, it must be killed, he insisted. No more discussion.

"Would you like me to call you a taxi," he asked in a warm, bloodless kind of way.

"Yes," my wife told him. "No," I said, worried the cab driver might be late and that he too would have to be killed. But no one heard me.

On the way to the bus station, way in the distance, I could hear the blood curdling screams of a cock.

"It's not that cock," my wife said. "They're not really going to kill the cock for waking us up too late. He was just saying all that to impress you. It's a cultural thing. They want us to come back." I didn't really disagree with her, but what about this idea of lateness, I wondered, and what could those so called other, various, capacities of lateness be?

On the bus to Vigo, a small boy sat on his mother's lap while the family chicken, looking half-starved, stood on the seat next to them. The boy kept pushing its head down, trying to get it to actually sit like everyone else because he heard, no doubt, the bus driver exclaim that unless everyone was sitting in their seats he would not move the bus. But the chicken resisted. It squirmed and began to flutter its wings. Things flew out of its wings that seemed to have their own wings from which other things flew and so on and so forth. The boy shouted something at it. Then his mother slapped the boy on the head and he started to cry.

"Can chickens sit?" I asked my wife.

"No," she said. Just like that. "No." "And besides, she said. "It's not your concern."

The bus started to move. It moved slowly and cautiously, squeezing itself really, screeching endlessly it seemed, through the narrow tunnel of the parking garage from which, finally, it emerged unscathed into the blinding sunlight. The sunlight around here always seemed to be blinding, relentless, unforgiving, and brutal. Was that too a cultural thing? I wondered. I wanted it to be, but my wife insisted it was geographical.

"Cultural? Since when is the sun cultural? I'd advise you to stay focused."

From where I sat, the bus driver looked isolated and abandoned. There was great distance between him and the first row of seats. He intrigued me. I told my wife I'd like to speak to him, perhaps during our first stop.

"He-is-the-BUS-driver. And besides, he probably doesn't understand English."

I didn't disagree. At the first stop, I went up to him and said, "How many years have you been driving a bus?"

"Cuantos anos?" I asked while turning a phantom steering wheel. He just stared at me. He could have said, "No comprendo," but he just stared at me. Then I saw a picture of a woman and two young children swinging precariously just above his rear view mirror.

"They're very beautiful," I said pointing to the picture.

"Ah," he sighed like a dying wave for which there is no return.

I was thrilled. We had bonded. Then he said, "We must leave now," and then I said, "Tengo calor," as if the heat or the fact or at least the idea or suggestion of the heat, might keep him talking to me, but instead he began to loosen the screws of his seat so that he could bounce on it more freely while listening to disco music along the long stretches of highway.

When I returned to my seat, I noticed that the seat the chicken had been sitting on, or whatever chickens do when presented with a seat, was empty.

"What happened to the chicken?" I asked my wife.

"The woman took it into the bathroom," she said. "I think."

"And then what?" I asked, because the woman and her child were there, fast asleep, but there was no chicken.

"I don't know," she said.

I wanted to wake the woman, or even the child and ask what happened to the chicken, but my wife was not wrong; it was not my concern. Besides, I was quite elated to have spoken, albeit quite briefly, to the bus driver, having apparently affected him so deeply, so suddenly, that a whole side of him, psychologically speaking, and hitherto suppressed, was seeping slowly out of him.

"Notice how funny, rather how strange, the bus driver is acting," I told my wife.

"What did you say to him?" she asked.

"Nothing," I said. "Just how beautiful his children were."

"How would you know?" she asked.

"He has their picture above the steering wheel. Them and his wife."

"You're going to kill us all," she said. "You've made him think about things too much."

After a while my wife and I got very hungry. We thought lunch was included in the trip. Little yellow substance-like sandwiches on the bus the travel agent told us were included in the package. We would not have come here without some package deal. We wouldn't have budged an inch without a package deal. The agent knew that. It was like yesterday. We were sitting in her office back in New York. She was looking at something on her computer and suddenly said, "Yup. They serve little finger sandwiches on the bus to Vigo. Sandwiches pequenas. It's right there." We believed her. We felt no need to crane our necks and stare into her computer screen. Why would she lie about something like that? No, if anything, the package lied. If they lied about the sandwiches what other lies might be out there waiting for us?

I had just started to doze off when the woman with the small boy and the chicken began to scream. "Mi Pollo! Mi Pollo!" I understood enough Spanish to figure out the third or fourth time she screamed out that, apparently, the chicken had escaped. But how? Where?

The driver stopped the bus in the middle of the highway. He walked back to where the woman was sitting. They talked for a long time before I realized the bus wasn't moving at all, that in fact it was the bus driver who needed to do that, to move it, and here he was talking endlessly to a woman about her missing chicken.

I looked at my wife and she was asleep. I wanted to wake her, to tell her we had to go, that we should get out now, that we should call the agency and complain, but about what? Being misled? Of course, after all, what was this chicken nonsense all about? There were chickens everywhere. Since when was a chicken ever singled out as special?

It seemed like hours, the heat was unbearable; the bus was filling up with cigarette smoke; I could swear too that it had started to groan as if it had to endure not only bad internal suspension but metaphysical pain as well.

The woman would not be consoled. Suddenly a great shout was heard and then a prolonged roar. They were bicyclists speeding past us on the highway. Crowds were gathered along the sides of the road. It made me think about life again, about movement, that things could move if they wanted to if there was enough interest and support, if crowds roared, urged us on, we could move towards our destinations, whatever they may be—but in the bus, we were lifeless, dead, stillborn, really. The bus driver, missing his wife and children and unborn child no doubt stood helpless before the verbal onslaught of the chicken woman. No one else said a word as if something like this happened all the time, as if they had all the time in the world, as if to arrive was simply to arrive, as leaving was simply to leave and nothing else, no expectation, no anxiety, no one waiting, or at least someone waiting who did not mind waiting or who might think to themselves, "it must be a chicken problem" and be completely content with that.

When my wife awoke, she asked, quite seriously, "Where are we?" as if we had been moving the whole time. When I explained to her that we hadn't moved for hours, she shook her head and had this disgusted look on her face like it was I who should have done something about that.

We were supposed to meet some friends in Vigo that afternoon, but now it looked like we'd never make it. I wondered if this chicken problem would be one of those "other capacities of lateness" the hotel manager had talked about, but our friends were not the kind of people who might think "this might be a chicken problem," and then keep waiting. They were not people who took waiting lightly. They themselves were always late and expected you to wait for them, but the reverse was not true. But just as I was thinking this, I felt the bus move; actually jolt an inch or two forward and then stop, as if the driver tried to catch the bus by surprise, and the bus, catching on, refused to move. That was when the driver got off the bus and never came back.

It's true he never did come back, but that's not to say we didn't all go after him, especially the woman with no chicken, who was immediately drawn to the driver's sudden escape, to the urgency of his leaving, to the desperation in the way he manually opened the mechanical doors, leapt off his seat and disappeared so utterly and completely into the blinding light of day. She herself was in a restrained state of urgency and desperation for hours now. It seemed everyone was, including us.

"Mi pollo! Mi pollo!" she cried again as if suddenly remembering her chicken was gone, truly gone and that the driver's leaving had something to do with this, either by leaving he was going off to find them or by leaving he was absconding with it, perhaps in his pants or under his shirt.

"What's with that woman?" I asked my wife.

"What's with that driver?" she asked in turn. I didn't disagree with her.

People were starting to wiggle around in their seats now and then many in window seats began to crane their necks to see where the driver and the woman might be going. There was a wooded area just off the road. Perhaps it was in there, in those woods where people went to find lost things, I thought.

When after several minutes the bus driver had still not returned, my wife and I started this conversation that I had never expected to have. The thing was I can go a long time, months, even years thinking everything was all right, that things were going along quite smoothly that the only person who might possibly be suffering some sort of spiritual or emotional discomfort might be me, but as it turned out, as the conversation went on, I began to learn more and more about my wife's own spiritual and mental discomforts, about her dissatisfaction with things, in particular me, things I had never imagined.

"You're the one who planned this package," I said.

"That's the thing," she said. "I'm the one who always has to plan everything. Everything is always dumped in my lap. And you're always tired. There was more life in that chicken than there is in you."

I didn't know whether to agree with her or not. I have to admit, though, that lately I was feeling pretty lifeless.

"Well, maybe so," I said, but how did I know we'd have a restless bus driver, a driver torn by guilt and regret, a driver who abandoned his pregnant wife and children to get this bus to Vigo on time?"

"How did you know that?" my wife asked.

"He told me..."

"He never told you."

"Then I must have dreamt it," I said.

"You certainly sleep enough to dream a lot of things, but I don't think you dreamt this."

"Then how would I know?"

"That's what you want to have happened. That's what you wish for yourself."

"It is?" I asked.

"Of course it is," she said. "Don't you know that?"

Again, maybe it was, so I didn't know whether to agree with her or not.

Then we all left the bus. Every last one of us. We finally had to. A policeman or traffic director, someone in an official looking uniform who seemed to appear out of nowhere, popped his head in the bus and shouted like in a nightmare where the voice is too big for the person's mouth and seems to be coming from several different directions at once.

"Out! Out! Everyone out!"

The chicken lady, of course, was the first to go. On my way out, I looked under every seat but could find no sign of her chicken. I wanted to be a hero and find the chicken. Probably to show my wife I was capable of action. Yes, I would find the chicken cowering and ruffled under a seat, lift him above my head and cry out to the multitudes, "El Pollo! Yo Tengo el Pollo!" And the woman would run to me and lift her arms above my head to get her chicken and then she'd kiss the chicken a thousand times and perhaps curse at it a thousand more and finally she would look at me like the savior, like Jesus himself, and bow to me, and kiss my feet, and whatever else she felt compelled to do, but alas, there was no chicken hiding anywhere but only crumpled, yellow-stained napkins, crushed and discarded paper cups, bread crumbs, all looking suspiciously like the aftermath of that package deal we were promised yet never received. No, I couldn't find a single chicken feather anywhere, and so, like everyone else, I was destined to leave the bus empty handed and hero-less.

Once off the bus, we heard the distant cries of a baby. It was coming from the woods. We all walked quietly into the woods as if we were being led there even though it didn't look like there was anyone leading us. Perhaps it was the child's cries themselves that led us. My wife looked at me, not with her usual disapproval but with a kind of hopefulness like maybe...maybe...just maybe...maybe...but maybe what? I remembered then about the miscarriage. There was a short interval right before that of cautious joy and then an even shorter one of fear and a gnawing sense of inevitability and finally, a slightly longer one of hopelessness and despair. This was all in a matter of days. Afterwards we said nothing to each other and decided to go to Spain with the money we saved on clothes and a nursery.

The crying grew louder, stronger, more urgent. The bus passengers among us were chattering rapidly, old men and women were beating their chests. Children laughed and screamed and kicked up clouds of dust that obscured our vision.

Having our vision obscured was good, however, because it gave everything a sense of other-worldliness, kind of a void between the real and unreal, a little darkness before the clearing, some breathing space before what I felt to be an unavoidable collision course with fate. I could feel the heaviness in the air, in my legs, my brain. At last came a clearing, of dust, of forest, and there stood, as if smack against our faces, a dilapidated shack, some unlivable structure from which, nevertheless, emanated the sounds of new and vital life.

"Should we go inside?" I asked my wife.

"Of course," she said as if it were quite obvious we should, as if it were fated we should be here, at the threshold of this particular shack, at this particular moment, as if life might suspend itself until we entered. And why wouldn't I know that?

Inside there was the smell of rotting flesh and dying vegetation. We were not surprised. At first we saw nothing or perhaps too much so we followed the eyes of the others and there at the back of the shack was our bus driver holding a tiny baby above his head, a young woman lying on a bed of straw, two small children, a half—starved chicken, the woman who owned the chicken, and her little boy. Suddenly, the crowd, the very passengers whom the driver had abandoned, who had only just entered the shack, began to chant, "Milagro! Milagro! Milagro!" They seemed to sense something special had happened. I envied having that sense of knowing something special has happened without actually having to see it happen. Then, without directions from anyone, they began to move closer and closer towards the child, stretching out their arms, their fingertips, trying to touch the baby as the bus driver raised it higher and higher above his head.

Someone grabbed my hand. It was my wife. I could feel the callous on her left index finger, the same callous I kept staring at the night we lost the baby, kept staring at the whole time she was losing the baby as if there had been nothing else to see or feel in the whole world. And now in this dilapidated old shack whose walls dripped with some sickly yellow substance, a crowd of abandoned bus passengers chanted "Milagro! Milagro!" as the driver lifted his child higher and higher above his head, always just beyond their reach, and a woman, who for the first time I noticed had egg blue eyes, held out her half-starved chicken to the crowd, begged them to touch it, and cried out in agony when no one would.

And all this time my wife held my hand and I could still feel the callous but it was different this time because I did not only feel the callous—I could feel my wife too—Yes, I could feel her whole hand, and not just the callous, pulling me out of the shack.

"Let's go," she said. "It's getting late."

I did not disagree.

"You're right," I said as we came out into a blinding sun. "It's getting very late."

We took a bus back to where we had started. We crossed to the other side of the road and took a bus going in the opposite direction. It was the only direction buses would be going until the next day when they'd go the other way again and we would try once again to get to Vigo.

We were back in the same hotel. The manager apologized for our inconvenience but because of such late notice he had to raise the price of our room. We called our friends in Vigo and told them we had a slight "chicken problem," and when there was no response, we said that we had also witnessed a miracle which we would tell them about the next day.

Then they said, "All right, then...we'll wait."

The next morning the cock crowed too early, at least earlier than I would expect a cock to crow.

"Do you think it's the same cock as last time?" I asked my wife.

"No," she said. "It wouldn't make sense. It must be a different cock."

"You mean they killed it," I said.

"No," she said. "Just a different one."

"Why?" I said. "It could be the same one but just frightened this time, afraid to fail."

My wife didn't exactly disagree, but she said, "Why should it be afraid? A cock is a cock. I think you might be giving it too much credit in the scheme of things."

I didn't disagree with her and the whole time we talked it was still very dark outside, and inside too, and soon we stopped talking, but the cock kept crowing until just before the sun rose.

Dream Of an Old Man On a Bicycle

Someone is telling me to go into the intersection, to cut a beautiful, passionate arc through traffic. I stop the bicycle, temporarily holding up traffic to take out a huge book on arcs, some perfect, some imperfect, some passionate, others merely efficient, some in color, some in black and white.

There's a large brown envelope stuck on page 2000. The flap or mouth of the envelope is beginning to unravel; the gum is drying up; the envelope is beginning to open before my eyes. A light, a very powerful light emanates from inside. I avert my eyes now; the pain of the light, far greater than daylight, is too much for my eyes to bear and then I realize I only have one eye, one eye in order to make that perfect arc across traffic and I'm not certain now that it's possible though I do have the memory of two eyes, the memory of the first eye that floats in its socket like a dead fish in a lily pond. This too is okay because on page 2012, there is a section on arcs made with one eye, beautiful, lovely golden arcs that begin slowly, at ground level and then rise gradually until reaching itself, its own arc, its own rounded back of absolute perfection.

Of course, this is all theoretical. Someone from behind, another bicyclist waiting to move through, pushes against my rear, urges me on.

"But the envelope?" I ask him. "Arc or no arc, there is an envelope to deal with."

"Forget it," he says. "If it is meant to unravel, let it unravel. You cannot tamper with the way things are meant to be. That is the trouble with you young people; one eye or two eyes, you are all the same. Out to make trouble."

I am past 70 and nearly deaf and don't understand a damn thing he says but still I listen to his words very carefully. I do know that in my dreams everyone has one eye and everything has one side. There is no room for divergence or even thought.

So I begin to make my arc. It goes badly at first. I wobble across the intersection. Car horns blast at me from all sides. I look up, another dangerous action, an action unheard of in Chinese intersection crossing, yet I look up and notice one car, a van really in front of me. It is driven by a young Chinese man in an American baseball cap. He frightens me. However, I believe at this moment it is okay to be frightened; it is also okay to die. That is when I begin to look even beyond him to the people sitting in the back seat. I notice a Chinese baby being held by an American woman and next to her, an American man, most likely her husband who is frantically looking for something.

I seem distracted for a moment and begin to stumble again, just slightly, but enough to plunge just a bit towards the traffic, enough so to be crushed or severely wounded or at least to lose my other eye which if I am correct would make me completely blind and unable to support myself. However, I am able to right myself, though in doing so knock over several bicyclists behind me like so many dominoes. I see the American man now lean over to the driver, say something to him, directly into his ear as if not to take any chances. He seems desperate; part of me hopes this is life threatening, that they might need to turn back because he has lost or forgotten something that is a matter of life and death back at the hotel.

The baby seems to be staring at me now. Or do I give myself too much credit? All my life I have only been stared at in horror or out of a morbid curiosity, which in turn turns to pity or disgust. I believe the baby is staring only at the space in front of her, clogged now with various shapes and figures, dark and light, collectively or singly, though still, when all is said and done, I would have liked to think she were staring at me. Why not? Isn't there some kind of identification going on here, even if it is an identification with what I could have become? Just to make sure, I begin to move my dead eyeball around its socket, like magic, because babies like magic, to see if she reacts and yes, she begins to cry, in, for lack of a new word, horror. She notices me! This eyeball can do many things. It can make babies cry, it can stop traffic; it can turn a person's heart against oneself. Certainly it is a bad thing for China. It only re-affirms our backwardness, our lack of medical care, our total disregard for the crippled and deformed. I am very fond of this eye.

The woman now has an angry look on her face. She shakes her head at the back of her husband's head who is still speaking into the head of the young driver. It is head to head to head with not one person looking into another's eye except for the child and myself. I am feeling very confident now, that perhaps my one eye is as good as all their eyes put together. I feel something now, quite sticky against the palm of my hand. It is that ghastly envelope and now it has been sealed shut again with the sweat of my palm. I notice the horns have stopped blowing, that the cars have all stopped moving, that time has stopped, and they wait for me to complete my arc. I am thrilled. Perhaps this is my day after all.

I look at my watch and notice that beneath the shattered crystal my father and mother are dancing in a ballroom in Shanghai extremely handsome and beautiful unaware they are about to be bombed by the Japanese. Then I look at the front wheels of the van and notice how twisted they have become and then suddenly untwisted and then twisted again as if the driver is contemplating making a turn, his own imperfect arc into traffic—the American has stopped talking into the back of the driver's head and instead searches his bag again, frantically; I know the feeling, getting near the bottom of something, knowing in your heart there is nothing there, yet continuing to search nevertheless. It is the beauty and futility of hope put together.

I hear a mad dog now howling in the distance and wonder if it is not time to wake up, to end this dream before I'm sorry, before I do something I will regret, not so much to myself but to others, perhaps to the Americans and the Chinese baby in the van. I see the American shaking his head again from side to side, catastrophically; I've seen that very same shaking of the head during famines and floods and earthquakes or perhaps when a baby is returned to the orphanage for having too big a nose. Should I end his suffering, I wonder and give him the envelope for I know this is what he must be looking for. I feel it begin to unravel again. Perhaps the meaning of life is contained in this envelope, things like why one is given one eye in life and others two and so on and so forth, small mysteries like why some babies are adopted by rich western families while still others are returned when it is discovered that one of their eyes does not move or there is a slight dent in the head that cannot be undented.

This baby has two eyes that move like beautiful young tadpoles in her head. She looks at me with curiosity; I see how they strike out in the same direction, towards the corner of each socket and look suspiciously at me. She knows what I have done before I know it. She couldn't have known. She wasn't there. No one could have seen how quickly I had swept up the envelope at the train station's waiting room the day it fell out of the American woman's bag.

They were heading back to Shanghai. I remember sneaking up to the platform to warn them, to give them back their envelope. It looked important; perhaps they would take pity on me and find it in their hearts to take me with them. But once on the platform, without my broom, without my identity, there was no proof at all who I was. I was stopped by the railroad official who questioned my motives, why I was without a ticket and dressed so shabbily.

"I am not a passenger," I told him. "I am the broom man," but he called me a liar, an enemy of the state. He lashed into me with great, joyful abandon. His eyes were strong and wicked. Later, a woman joined him, a woman who looked like someone I had played with in my youth and did everything she could to torture me. From time to time, I looked over at the American couple and their guide, but they looked the other way; they looked desperately towards the train tracks. They felt not the slightest compassion for me. They just wanted to be gone, to forget any of this ever happened. Their heads were filled with visions of ancient gardens and temples, with wild names and esoteric poetry that fell arcless and unreachable into their hearts. Funny how rich ancient ghosts with two eyes are always treated better than those of us who are still alive but have only one.

When someone asked me what I wanted to be when I grew up I said, quite sincerely, "A ghost from the dead past." They wrote this down. I believe this was my progress report. In the long run, my broom would be confiscated. I would be abandoned again, thrown into the streets, forced to find shelter below the railroad tracks. The bicycle, of course, comes from nowhere. It exists only in the American's mind. I am his nightmare and though I try to make it as unpleasant as possible for him, I can just do so much in such foreign, unfamiliar territory.

When I look back into the van the American's head is missing. It is somewhere under the car seat, his hands now recklessly, with great abandonment, not aware of the great dangers that may lurk beneath that seat, flailing against the darkness, my darkness, the darkness, hot and filthy and stifling that I spent my first hours in, the better hours of my life I might say. I feel his hands, the violation, how many times have hands sought me out in just this way and then rising from the depths, the man still headless, the envelope, like some yellow sickly flag, the color of my own face when they finally dragged me out. He pulls it out like a reluctant fetus against its will from its dark fetid space and raises it above his severed head for his head remains under there. Has he discovered something else? Another child perhaps? I could have shown him so much, the passageways within the belly of the car, the tiny broken bones and half-formed spleens that were my only companions. Until one day I must have cried or said something perhaps inadvertently out of pure unconscious hunger licked the sweat off the heel of a foreigner, they swept me out. It was the broom I came to love, my father, my brother; I grew up sweeping out other babies from under the seats of private vans.

I look again at my envelope, as it continues to unravel. It has a life of its own and I can no longer stop it. When it is completely open I look inside and notice a sheet of American stamps. There is a note attached. "For Wei Mei—a wonderful guide—good luck in all your entrepreneurial endeavors—" I look back to the van and notice the Americans are all smiling. The man holds up the envelope. The van begins to pick up speed and I am forced to move again. However, I forget how to move. I remember movement has something to do with my legs and the bicycle on which they seem to be resting. I have forgotten everything. No, I never knew anything. That accounts, I believe, for the pureness of my feelings.

Of course, he is waking now. The flight attendant must be asking him if he wants domestic or foreign wine. With one eye open, he glimpses his child still asleep, breathing like a small frog under a lily pad.

As for me, my other eye is gone too. There is only darkness now, yet still I must finish my perfect arc. It is either that or be crushed to death. The occupants, the driver of the van, seem too ecstatic now, too full of hope, to stop anymore. If they must kill they will kill. Yes, I must continue my perfect arc and what better time then when I have forgotten everything, even how to move my legs.

I hear horns blasting, children crying, vendors screaming. But the sound begins to fade as I am lifted into the air. I hear the engines of a great bird screeching over China. I feel the back of my own arc rub against me. I smell baby powder. The last thing I smell is American baby powder. It is unmistakable. I have smelled it before. They bring it to the orphanage because they are warned over the e-mail about rashes, rashes everywhere, resistant to anything we have to spread over them. I still have that rash, of course and I see it now, a brilliant red streak across the dawn. Then I think to myself, but I'm wondering if it's not really him thinking to himself about what I might think, that wouldn't it be wonderful if when I finally dissolve, and I will dissolve shortly, if I can dissolve into the child's eyes. This might be asking for too much so I think it might be better to wait. But I must be patient, for waiting, I can feel now in my bones, is like eternity.